TAKE AIM

TRENCH RAIDERS BOOK 4

THOMAS WOOD

BOLEYNBENNETT PUBLISHING

Visit my website at www.ThomasWoodBooks.com

Printed in the United Kingdom

First Printing: March 2019
by
BoleynBennett Publishing

GRAB ANOTHER BOOK FOR FREE

If you enjoy this book, why not pick up another one,
completely free?

'Enemy Held Territory' follows Special Operations
Executive Agent, Maurice Dumont as he inspects the
defences at the bridges at Ranville and Benouville.
Fast paced and exciting, this Second World War thriller is
one you won't want to miss!
Details can be found at the back of this book.

1

My body twitched with every syllable of gunfire and every gut-wrenching thump of artillery that tolled across the chaotic patch of France that I stood in.

I could make out every single rifle crack, and each and every time that one of our boys ejected a round, as they swiftly pulled the bolts back on their rifles. They were doing a sterling job of holding back the German counter-attack, that was itself in reply to one of our own advances earlier on.

Our offensive had faltered, at the expense of hundreds, if not thousands, of young men's lives. It was a tactic that I was reluctantly used to by now, but one that was still excruciatingly painful to get my head around.

The sound of our artillery, pulverising just fifty yards in front of our wire, shook my insides as if I was lying on a train track, with an express train thundering right above my head. With each and every subsequent blast, that accompanied the screaming locomotives, I thought of the death and destruction that each shell would bring.

I had been on the end of them many a time myself, and did not envy the German soldier in the slightest who was now facing the onslaught of our field artillery. Before too long, I hoped anyway, the German counter-attack would be repelled, and the sounds of the screaming hell hounds overhead would slowly die away. So too with the incessant rattling of the defending machine guns, as they aimlessly fired into the mist, accompanied by the most sobering of thuds, as they tore their way through human flesh.

Once those sounds had vanished into nothing more than a mere memory, the gradual groans of the dying and wounded would permeate into the eternal memory of every soldier within earshot. That was the worst of all the noises on the Western front.

There was nothing that you could do about it, there was no ability to exercise compassion, as that so frequently resulted in a German round embedding itself right between your eyes. There was nothing anyone could do, apart from listen and pray that it would all end soon enough.

The sounds of men hollering at the top of their lungs as they surged towards where I was stood, but also as the Vickers guns continued to chatter away, suddenly brought me back to reality.

Everything around me that seemed capable of making even the slightest of noises seemed to do so, with each utterance apparently tightening its deathly grasp around my stomach. I felt the burning acid sloshing away around my insides, searing me more than a bullet ever could do.

As the noise and cacophony threatened to overwhelm me, I distracted myself by finally opening my eyes.

Quite instinctively, I slammed them tightly shut once again, as I took more comfort from the self-imposed darkness than I did from what I had seen.

I had seen bodies before, plenty of them in fact, and had in reality contributed my own fair share to the mountain of corpses that was growing every day in this war. But despite everything that I had done and seen, it is never human desire to see even more dead bodies than you strictly have to. Especially when those bodies are those of young men who should have no experience of death.

They were beginning to mount up throughout the frontline trench that I stood in, and the longer that I stood there the more vulnerable my ears became to hearing the flesh-ripping rounds entering their young bodies.

The sound of rifle fire, as it intensified and began to twang off bits of metal debris, that was meant to keep these young boys as safe as possible, began to resound even more than my own heartbeat.

"Left flank! Left flank! Take them, take them!" I desperately wanted to step up onto the fire step and see what it was that the NCO was screaming at, simultaneously wondering if he repeated everything that he said in his life twice.

Screams of, "I got him!" and "Keep going!" were interspersed with other screams of encouragement.

"They're on the turn!"

"Get back to where you came from, you rat!"

I listened to a hundred more such phrases, varying in their coarseness and pride at murdering another human being. But it took me a while to realise that one voice in particular was calling out to me.

"You there! Oi, you!"

"Sergeant! Are you with us?"

Finally, I opened my eyes for longer than half a second.

I was met by the stern gaze of a lieutenant who looked far too old to be carrying such a rank. His eyes were dark and mournful and the words that he spat at me reflected them as such.

"You are here to help, are you not?"

He knew that I was, I didn't need to be, but Captain Arnold did not like half-hearted volunteers. It was why we had all taken the white armband with an enthusiasm reserved only for him.

"Yes, Sir."

"Well get some of these boys on your stretcher then, will you? Get them away from here!"

He stood just a few yards away from me, but he still had to utilise all of his vocal chords just to be heard above the din.

The ground shook feverishly as I looked around for who I could take with me. As the small particles of dirt were disturbed from the walls of the trench, a corporal, who didn't look a day over the age of fifteen, stepped forward to helpfully point towards one of his wounded comrades.

"Take him. He copped a sniper round to his neck, I think."

I nodded to him, "Righto."

Unfolding the canvas stretcher so that we could get the injured boy on board, McKay and I began to unceremoniously heave the weight of a rapidly deteriorating comrade, so that we could get him somewhere a bit safer.

The boy had indeed been hit by a sniper, either that or it was an extremely lucky round that had sent him flying from the fire step. His neck had been opened up expertly, as if he had carved the wound himself to show something off proudly to us.

The back of his head too, began to leak a scarlet liquid into the surface of the canvas, as a head wound began to drain his body of his precious blood.

As we moved him, he began to flap around like a fish out of water, his arms jerking up and down as if he was trying to tell us something, his legs repeating the signal just in case we had missed it.

"Okay mate... Okay. Calm down, we are getting you out."

Suddenly, the young boy clamped his fist around McKay's lower arm and heaved himself up valiantly. He stared directly into my soul. In that moment I knew that he had seen every regret, every greedy moment, every selfish desire that I had ever harboured in my heart.

He had the most beautiful, captivating, hazel coloured eyes, which were as open and honest as a child's, as he continued to stare at me with his childlike belief that I would be able to rescue him from any situation.

I was dumbfounded and was grateful for the sudden reprieve as he softly blinked. When they reopened, I had still not recovered from the intense glare that he was delivering, and I could do nothing but stare at the gaping hole that had been forcibly ripped open at his throat.

I was thankful that McKay was there to share the moment with me.

"Okay, mate. Come on, let go. Then we can get you out of here. Come on."

His voice was uncharacteristically soothing, as he gently unwrapped the boy's fingers from around his forearm. The voice that I had come to know and love, like the sound of a boot crunching over gravel was gone, but it held fast and didn't crack or crumble, like I was certain my own would have done. McKay seemed confident, unaffected even.

It had been a long day, and it was only just after daybreak. It had all started in the early hours of the morning, when the hollers and shouts from outside the window of the *Café de Fleur* began to permeate into my unconscious mind.

"Get up, get up. Something's happening!" At first, the voice had sounded like it belonged to Bob Sargent, the man who had held my hand through my first few weeks on the frontline. But he was dead now, alive only in my dreams and thoughts.

As I slowly began to come round from my much-needed sleep, the figure of Bob Sargent slowly morphed in the darkness to the altogether more harrowing figure of Private David Hamilton.

"Sergeant, something has happened! Captain Arnold said we are to head to the frontline immediately."

He was excited, and I began to wonder how I had slept through such an exhilarating episode that Hamilton had apparently witnessed.

"Come on, Andrew. Move yourself."

As I watched McKay begin to dress, I realised that the

hubbub was genuine, and that we had indeed been ordered to make our way to the front.

It was meant to be our night off, but the midnight patrol out in No Man's Land had hit some kind of trouble and, judging by the scene that had met my eyes, they had hit a lot of it.

Every single man in the patrol was wounded in one way or another, certainly, half of them never even returned to our lines.

As we began to tend to the wounded, all the other soldiers around us hopped up onto the fire step, ready to beat an advancing German army away from our front door.

We had spent the rest of the dark hours ferrying wounded troops to awaiting wagons, which then bumped their way towards the hospitals behind the lines. The young boy hit through the neck by a sniper was just one casualty too far for me.

Voices began to shout from every direction, a few of them I even recognised, but most of them were already dead. No one seemed to talk to one another exactly, but seemed to take great comfort from their ability to make some sort of noise. It meant that they were still alive.

"Andrew? Andrew? Are you alright? Can you hear me?"

I locked eyes with McKay, as his mouth continued to move. Gradually, he began to realise that I could not hear him and so gave up trying to shout above the *rat-tat-tat* of the machine gun just fifteen yards away.

We stared at each other in much the same manner that the young boy had stared at each one of us, silently communicating with one another our gratitude and relief that it had been our night off.

Just as another few thousand shells howled, what felt like inches above our heads, we seemingly agreed that we were the lucky ones. This could have been us.

"Let's get this poor git away from here, shall we?"

The horrible coarse tones that he coughed from the back of his throat were back. That was the kind of normality that I had been craving ever since my early morning wake-up call.

I agreed, by picking up the wooden handles at the lighter end of the load, as my hands began to tremble ever so slightly.

I wondered, being the one who was leading the evacuation, if McKay could see the slight tremor in my wrists, and hoped that he might put it down to the fact that I was struggling to keep the weight from crashing down to the ground. But, deep down, I knew that he would know of the real reason for my shaking digits.

I needed some of that paraffin, desperately.

I really needed the comfort of my hip flask right now. *GRHMN.*

2

McKay and I continued to ferry men on stretchers for a considerable amount of time, before we got any semblance of a break. Even then the break consisted of nothing more than a swift gulp of water, a few puffs on a cigarette and a much-needed glug from my hip flask.

"Let's get back to it, then."

I was in no state of mind to be the one taking charge right now, which was why I was incredibly grateful to have McKay by my side once again. It had felt like he had been beside me for a lot longer than he was in reality, and I found myself at regular intervals seeking him out, so that I could take some sort of comfort from his small, but powerful frame.

It was as if that the way he fought, with a viciousness and fury, would somehow rub off onto me, and if it didn't, then having him by my side might just be the key to making it home alive.

I turned to look at him as he called out my name, wondering what it was I had done wrong this time that he was pulling me up for. But as I looked at him, I realised that he was as surprised to see me looking round at him, as I was to hear his voice. As I stared at his face questioningly, the voice appeared again, but this time McKay's lips did not move.

"It was your fault, Andrew. Your fault."

My eyes narrowed slightly as I tried to figure out what exactly was going on, before spinning on my heel to try and locate the spectral voice. But there was no one else around who could speak in such a low tone and still be heard, especially as the field artillery were doing their utmost to deafen absolutely everyone in this little part of France.

I felt like talking back but was acutely aware of the inquisitive looks that I was drawing, not just from McKay, but the other men around me who had seen me stop dead in my tracks, to turn and confront a silent companion.

Then, the voice spoke again.

"Andrew. It was your fault. You hit me."

I had not expected to hear his voice ever again, that is generally how it goes when you witness someone dying. For a moment however, I was comforted by the genteel tones of Bob Sargent's voice, as they slithered their way into my mind. He spoke forcefully, like he so often did when he addressed me, but that sense of feeling like I was being reprimanded was all I had come to know of him in the last few weeks of his life.

He went to speak again but, before he could, he was cut short by the screaming and shouting of other stretcher bearers, as they thundered their way over the duck boards, racing to get their casualty to some sort of assistance.

"Stand back! Make way!" Bellowed the first stretcher bearer, his companion's face an apologetic one as he zipped past us standing in the mud.

"You're still needed up there!" he gasped as he stumbled his way past us.

It was stating the obvious, but one that made us fly through the trenches, skidding left and right, faster than we had done before.

We thumped into bodies running this way and that, who were grabbing vital bits of equipment that were needed to keep other boys alive, but also keep the Germans out. The Vickers guns seemed to glow red hot as they unceasingly spat round after round from the barrel of their weapons. They seemed quite well protected from where I stood, nothing more than a letterbox in amongst all the sandbags, for the barrel to poke out of and sweep No Man's Land. But the man feeding the monster, that cut down so many of the enemy, had a large gash just above his eyebrow, which had started to dribble down the side of his face.

No one, no matter how powerful they felt, was invincible here.

Catching sight of us, he turned his body to face us, still expertly feeding the canvas belt into the Vickers.

"We've got them on the run! They're falling back!"

I wished I shared his enthusiasm and optimism, but before I could say anything in reply to him a terrifying whistle filled my ears. He had heard it too and he adjusted his body to reflect that.

The high-pitched screaming of incoming artillery was

a noise that I would have been happy to have never heard ever again. But, for the rest of my days, I knew that it would haunt me every time I tried to fall asleep. Right there and then I promised to myself, that if I ever made it out alive of this war, I would pray a prayer of gratitude for every day that I did not hear shrieking shells.

The grin that had been chiselled into the face of the machine gunner was suddenly wiped clean, as a shell burst just in front of his position, dislodging some of the sandbags that surrounded the Vickers. He began to pull and push them around, to be able to get the gun back into operation again, but he hadn't realised that the man who sat next to him depressing the trigger, was dead.

As I watched him struggle, the thought came to me of the saying that you never hear the shell that hits you, and as I made my way over to the floundering machine gunner, I realised that the wise old NCOs who had uttered such words were correct.

I felt weightless for a moment, like you do when you dive into a lake and allow yourself to just float to the surface. I was peaceful for an instant, as I recalled my childhood days of swimming with the sister that I had long since forgotten. I would rise to the surface gracefully, arms and legs stretched out wide and taking in the muffled sounds of the water as the sediment settled at the bottom once more.

My sister would jump in beside me, invariably catching a toe or two as she endeavoured to destabilise my Lily pad impression. As I flew through the air, I began to realise how much I missed her, the guilt creeping in about how infrequent I had been in my reminiscences of her. Maybe I would write her a letter after this was all over.

As I gracefully stretched my arms and legs out to recreate my childhood folly, I realised that it was not my sister that was splashing into the water next to me, but the far more dangerous and unwelcome slams of four-two shells.

I hit the back of the trench wall, before sliding down it pathetically, crumpling in a heap on the floor. The machine gun nest had been vaporised completely, there was nothing there that indicated its prior existence, except a tangled mess of metal and a faint hint of the canvas belt that was being fed into its stomach.

The clouds above me seemed to darken as they rolled overhead, a mixture of the smoke that constantly clung to the air and the pessimism that was housed in the pit of every soldier who lived near this frontline.

I blinked furiously as I stared to the sky, fixing my eyes on a lighter patch of cloud, where I was certain that the sun was hiding behind. I willed it to emerge, even for half a second, just to kiss my skin and warmly make me feel like everything was going to be okay again.

But the longer I lay there, the more desperate my eyes became to close, and I found myself fighting furiously just to stay conscious.

I felt no pain, apart from that which was experienced when the dirt began its pitter patter to the ground and found its way into my eyes.

My arms and legs were numb, and for a few moments I panicked at the thought that I was nothing more than a torso and head. It felt like an almost ridiculous thought, and it was one that I would never have entertained had I not seen what I had done in the last four months of being a soldier.

I had seen men surviving with no arms, no legs and even with large portions of their head missing, for minutes after they had sustained their injuries. Maybe, I thought, that was what I was experiencing now, that feeling of serenity and peace that so many spoke of, that apparently came before you close your eyes for eternity.

Quite quickly, I realised that I wasn't about to die, or at least I still had my legs, as I could feel someone standing on them. Intuitively, my arms began to waft them away like a wasp, which only filled me with a little bit more reassurance that I was going to be fine.

"Oi, get off, will you?"

The figure staggered around for a second, surprised to hear a voice and find himself standing on top of me.

"Oh, sorry Sarge..."

The fear that rattled the boy's voice spurred me on as I shot to my feet, checking myself over for any signs of my own blood.

I looked around at the carnage that the direct hit had brought, whilst simultaneously looking around to see if I could see McKay. I needed him by my side.

"Where's your rifle, Private?"

The boy fumbled around before producing it, "Here it is, Sergeant."

"Well get up where that Vickers was, and make sure none of the Boche try to sneak through, will you?"

"What, on my ow... Yes Sergeant."

He had quickly looked around him and seen that there was hardly a platoon of enthusiastic soldiers ready to reinforce him. Someone would be along to kneel down beside him soon enough, there was bound to be an officer issuing orders somewhere.

In the meantime, I had a bigger priority, I needed to find McKay. I began to scrabble around in the dirt heaving at great mounds of hardened rock, not even registering how heavy and cumbersome each of them was. Such was my desperation to find Fritz.

I began uncovering bodies of deceased soldiers, who I could do nothing for, apart from simply leaving them to their rest. Muddied palms lay upturned to the sky as they reached out to me to pull them away, which I did. That was until however, I realised that the palm had not been McKay's, and so left them to fend for themselves.

Just as I was beginning to lose all hope, I heard a croaking voice from somewhere behind me. A Scottish voice.

"Andrew..."

I scanned the muddied and bloodied figures that were dotted all around the dugout, before my eyes fell on one that I vaguely recognised, the whites of his eyes burning brighter than the North Star.

"Ellis..."

"I've got you, I'm coming Fritz."

The lower half of his body was completely submerged, and I began digging away at him like a dog retrieving a buried bone. Eventually, I felt like I was getting somewhere.

"Give me some of that," he rasped trying to point towards my chest. Quickly, I gave him a sip from my hip flask, before pulling the last few lumps of dirt from his ankles.

"Are you hurt? Can you walk?"

"Yes… I think so, I'll give it a try anyway."

He began hauling himself to his feet, like a new-born calf, before swaying on the spot slightly as he regained his composure.

Men began to groggily come round, instinctively retaking their position up on the fire step, as they awaited the return of the enemy. Others, failed to get up, the lucky ones managing to let a groan pass over their lips in exasperation.

"Let's find ourselves an alive one, Fritz."

"Where's the stretcher? It's gone."

"We don't need one, unless you want to tell his mum that was the reason that you couldn't get him out?"

He thought about it for a moment, "That one, over there. I'm having his legs though."

"Pathetic."

3

As soon as we had grabbed the body that McKay had pointed to, the boy began screaming so loud that it must have been heard as far as Paris. To begin with neither of us had any idea what he was screaming about, and so opted to simply ignore him.

But slowly, my ears began to tune into his voice, as we shook the poor fellow around, and we charged towards help.

"My rifle! I need it! Now!"

The poor man was in no fit state to be in charge of a colony of lice, never mind the commander of a life-taking rifle. From what I could see, he had been shot somewhere in his back, the blood leaking so profusely from his lumbar region that it began to soak through the canvas of the stretcher within minutes, like some grotesque filtration process.

The agony that he was in was etched across his face, and I felt every bump and groove with him, as he subjected me to the pain through his bellows. His legs bucked and kicked sporadically into the air and it was almost as if he was about to spring up and sprint to the aid station himself.

"I'll go and look for it in a minute, mate. Let's just get you onto the truck first." I tried to sound as soothing as I possibly could, as we slid his stretcher next to three others who were all eerily silent, as if they had already given up.

"You really shouldn't lie to them like that," rebuked McKay, as we lead our aching and frail bodies back towards the frontline once more. "You shouldn't give them false hope."

"Come on Fritz, he's not going to know any different. The poor lad's probably going to be dead before they even switch the engine."

McKay went to rebuff my claims, before another timid voice entered the fray.

"You two, any chance of hopping on and helping us at the field hospital? They're completely overwhelmed."

We looked at each other for half a second, before the same thought flashed across both our minds.

There was almost always a nice cup of coffee in it for us if we were polite to one of the nurses.

Silently, we answered the man's question and, with his help, we hauled ourselves up onto the back of the truck, next to the man still screaming for his rifle.

The journey itself was not a long one, but it was made longer by the man's insistence on calling out for every person that he had ever met in his life. It was a pitiful sight to see, as he reeled his way through the names, gradually realising that not one of them was coming to his aid and even if they did, there was not a lot that they would be able to do for him.

It almost came as a relief when he breathed his last. At least that way McKay and I could enjoy something resembling silence.

"He dead?"

I nodded a reply to the chubby little orderly as he made his way to the back of our truck. He didn't look too much of a bad character at first glance, but the man had such an air of foulness, that I could not help but hate everything about him. He looked both McKay and me up and down, as if he had never seen such a deplorable case of human beings, before muttering a few more words, which seemed like he was degrading himself even further.

"Over there. Behind that row of tents. You should know where to put him."

McKay looked squarely at me as if to say, "What have we done to offend him?" I shrugged my shoulders and pulled a face, as the orderly turned away from us screaming at the top of his lungs.

"Over here! Two more cases for Captain Saunders!"

Like a pair of schoolboys who had just received the cane, we did what we were told to the letter, carefully removing the stretcher from the back of the truck and heading towards the row of tents that he had pointed to.

"Poor boy probably died thinking that you were going to look for his rifle," McKay mumbled with an air of accusation. "You lied to him."

"Or," I offered, "he died believing that he was soon going to be reunited with the one thing that matters to all of us. Maybe I gave him hope."

"Doubt it. Don't think there's any of that left anywhere near here."

"That's true."

We stopped talking to one another, as we both registered the smell around about the same time, the stench so putrid that even uttering a single syllable threatened to produce plentiful supplies of vomit.

For some reason, we seemed to speed up the closer we got to it, a naivety encompassing us both when we really should have known what to have expected.

There was row upon row of bodies, all laid out in single file, as if in some horrific waiting line to gain entry through the pearly gates. They were neatly spread, as if they had chosen their own little patch of ground themselves, with just enough room on either side of them for someone to gently manoeuvre down if needed.

A brave priest was confronting the smell head on, as he prayed a blessing over each of the deceased men before moving on to the man next to him.

Bit late for that now.

"Place him down over there, please. At the end of that row. Take him off the stretcher first." The nurse that addressed us was pleasant, her face pretty enough to distract us from the commanding tones that she spoke to us in. No sooner had she given us direction than she was busying herself by removing certain personal artefacts that had been cruelly separated from their masters.

We did as we were told, softly placing the young boy down next to the body of an ageing Sergeant who bore a striking resemblance to myself. I stared at him for a few moments, part of me even wishing that it was in fact my own corpse that I looked at and not just one of a doppelgänger. He was lanky and slim, and I could tell even in death that his chest would bend outwards proudly, if he had the ability to stand again.

Despite the blood that trickled down the side of his face, he looked reasonably well rested which was where the similarities between me and the deceased man ended. It had been a while since I had looked in a mirror, the last time that I had done, the huge dark bags that clung to the underside of my eyes had started to look like I had been in a pub brawl, the stress lines etched across my forehead doing nothing to help me look my best.

"The stretcher, gentlemen. Take it over to the next truck that's heading back to the frontline." The nurse barely looked up from her duties.

"Yes, miss," I croaked obligingly, as we were all subjected to the orderly screaming once again.

"Don't know about you," said McKay overwhelmed with discontentment, "but I don't much fancy going talking to that orderly again. Do you?"

"I didn't mind him actually. He reminded me of you."

"Get off... He's not nearly good-looking enough."

"Back to Porky Paul's?" I suggested.

Within half an hour, we were staggering through the door and into the quaint little café owned by the over-weight Frenchman. Even as the door slammed shut behind us the noises that bellowed in my head did not dwindle at all, if anything, all they did was reach a climax.

"Ah, boys. My boys!" The Frenchman's unnecessarily loud voice did nothing to soothe my headache, and would become another of the continual sounds that echoed around the void in my brain for hours to come.

His intentions were good, very good, as he quickly produced two glasses and automatically began to fill them in front of our appreciative eyes. He hummed and whistled as he did so, with no tune in particular, alternating between an upbeat mumbling and a melancholic whistle, which had begun to annoy McKay before he had even started doing it.

As Porky Paul went to leave our table, McKay suddenly gripped his bottle-wielding arm.

"Leave that here, would you?" He said without looking at Paul, instead choosing to stare at the ground between them.

"But, my friend, I have other customers other than you. What will they drink?"

McKay flicked his head up to look straight at Paul and repeated his request.

"Leave the bottle here, Paul."

Suddenly, the rest of his customers didn't matter, as the solid base of the bottle smashed down hard on the surface of our table. Soon, my headache would be gone, and I wouldn't be caring about anything that I'd seen.

I allowed him a few seconds to return to room temperature before quipping, "I hope you're paying for that."

He raised half an eyebrow as he laid a deck of cards out on the table, "I normally do."

As we spent the next hour or so shuffling and dealing cards, Porky Paul needn't have worried about what his other customers might drink, as there weren't any. The café was normally a hub of activity and joviality but today, it was the total opposite.

It was melancholic, depressing even, as each man in

there sought only to drink away his problems and his recollections. The walls all around me seemed to be painted a darker shade of grey than they normally were, and the flakes that were falling from the ceiling doing so in a much more suicidal fashion than I'd ever noticed.

The only men that were in there were the ones that had already done their duty and could no longer stomach the scenes of defeat that we had been subjected to for the last six or seven hours. The midnight patrol that had stumbled into all kinds of trouble, should have been a deterrent for the offensive that was planned to take place, but for whatever reason it was ignored.

The advance had ultimately faltered, and I thought back to the time when I had gone over the top, and I had seen most of my platoon completely wiped from the face of the earth in a matter of moments. I was certain that there would be more than one or two boys who felt the same that morning, but at the same time I felt like I was the only man in the boat.

Le Plantin was completely deserted, with only a few runners screeching through the village to make it to HQ a mile or so further down the road. Everyone else had left for the front almost immediately, to help in any way that they could and provide assistance to the dying.

Gradually, our game of cards went from two participants to three and finally to four, as Hamilton and Earnshaw joined us respectively. For an hour, maybe longer, we mindlessly slapped cards down on the table, playing a game that only McKay really knew how to play. But after all, it was his deck of cards that we always played with.

I looked at each of their faces, and was hit by an overwhelming sense of affection for the men that were frequently asked to die alongside me, three or four times a week. Each one of the faces that my eyes fell upon were dishevelled, and even though they were clean and freshly shaven, each was scarred by the proximity to death that we always found ourselves in.

As I began to marvel at the way that Hamilton's eyes seemed to sink even further into the back of his head than normal, the Captain skulked in, forcing the door open so quickly that it smashed into the wall on the other side and rebounded with a crash.

Everyone, particularly Porky Paul, looked up with a jump.

"You lot. Upstairs, now."

As one, we looked at each other surprised. He never spoke to us like that, not even when we were in a shell hole with a German patrol just inches away from our head. He never got that flustered.

"What's possessed him?" Earnshaw said, revealing his hand to us.

"Must be something that you've done, Harry," I offered. "No one else can wind him up like that."

4

We shuffled into the tiny upstairs room, that Porky Paul had graciously given us the run of many months ago now. It was the first time that I realised how unremarkable a room it was, and it was the closest thing that I had to home.

The walls had once been a creamy colour but were now damp and slowly surrendering to the mildew, that grew in the corners of the room, and clung to our chests while we sat there. The beds, which were pushed to the outer walls during the day, were messy and unmade, with everything from books to half eaten cans of bully beef sitting on top of pillows.

It seemed like it was the only time that each of us had taken any notice of the room that we all slept in, as we continually stared at the floor boards, not wanting to be the first man to make eye contact with the Captain.

It was the first time that I'd seen the Captain properly angry, I had never before heard him address us with such anger and frustration in his voice. Which was saying something, as we had been through a lot together.

As a group, we naturally formed a semicircle around Captain Arnold, as if it was any other normal briefing. But this time we all kept a larger distance between us and him than we would normally have dared. It was almost as if none of us wanted to be in range of one of his fists.

The Captain began pacing up and down before us, from left to right, spinning around on his heel while he pinched at his forehead and rummaged through his hair.

As if he needed reminding that we were there, I spoke up.

"Sir?"

He looked up, "Ah... Yes. Right."

He placed his palms together, as if he was about to say a prayer, but instead pushed his index fingers into the bridge of his nose, like he was concentrating hard on what he was about to say.

"Take a seat, gents. Sit down."

It was as if the twenty seconds that it had taken him to bound up the stairs had calmed him somehow, and he was now the normal Captain that we all knew and respected. It restored some of the trust that we had in him to the point where we felt confident he wasn't about punch one of us square in the face.

"We are... We..." He took a few more seconds to try and compose himself to formulate the sentences in his own mind. It was a moment where we all took the opportunity to look at one another and wonder what it was that had the Captain as flustered as he was.

"We are being moved away. To another sector altogether. You can say goodbye to this café for now, quite possibly forever. Any friends that you have here, including women, are to be bid farewell to, immediately. You will not be able to talk to them again."

We all sat completely dumbfounded for a few seconds, before Hamilton had the confidence to speak up on behalf of all of us.

"But where, Sir? And why?"

The Captain chose to answer the first part of Hamilton's query, but noticeably failed to answer the second, the one that we were all far more intrigued with.

"We are being moved to the Somme sector. Near a town called Albert. They've seen a lot of action recently, and now the powers that be have decided that we should go there too."

"Well, what is there that we haven't seen already?" questioned an irate McKay. All that he was met with was a lingering silence, an uneasy one.

My stomach began gurgling at the news and I shifted warily on my feet, in case any of the others heard it and mistook it for fear. Throughout my whole time in the team, I tried my absolute hardest to give off an image of courage and bravery, but deep down I was petrified, never more so than when we were told we would be moving to Albert.

"Sir," I croaked, "why exactly are we going to Albert? It's not like they are overstaffed here, am I right in saying?"

The Captain finally perched on the end of one of the flimsy but surprisingly comfortable beds, wiping the palm of his hand down the length of his face.

"It's because..." His voice was tremulous and weary, a complete contrast to how it had sounded the first time that I had met him. When I had met Terence Arnold some five months previous, his voice was clear and proud, as if it had been tuned to perfection by an aristocratic tuning fork. But now it was as if it had been knocked from its pedestal, an element of doubt and fear now creeping in just at the edges, just enough for his Sergeant to realise how fragile he was becoming.

"Christopher, I'm... I'm sorry." For a moment I looked about the room trying to work out if he was talking to us or some apparition that had just stood next to him. It was only when McKay began to shuffle from side to side next to me that I remembered he even had a Christian name.

"What is it, Sir?" muttered McKay responding for the first time in years to how his mother had addressed him.

"Someone... Someone found out..." The Captain sighed and left his head resting in his hands, so heavily that I thought he would never be able to lift it up again.

"Found out about what?" mumbled Hamilton, the inexperienced and most recent addition to our team. The rest of us need not ask such a question, as we knew full well what the Captain had alluded to. It was something that not one of us had mentioned since the day that it had happened.

"Found out about what?!" demanded Hamilton this time, growing frustrated with the pale and shocked faces that he found himself staring at.

"Fill him in, Sergeant."

I was not one to disobey an order, but this was one that I was going to struggle to fulfil. With a weakness flooding my voice, I began to relay the story to Hamilton about how McKay had once considered desertion.

It was not a tale of courage or pride, but one of desperation and shame, one that enshrouded us all as individuals, but also as a team.

With every word that I uttered, I saw McKay's head sink down further and further with embarrassment, and I considered on more than one occasion of giving up completely, as I saw how much it was wounding my best friend with every syllable that I uttered.

"... He never went through with it of course. But it was something that we agreed should be kept silent out of the fear of what the repercussions might be. And now, it is coming back to haunt us."

Hamilton digested this latest bit of news, before angrily spewing his hot words into the room.

"And no one thought that I was worthy of knowing this? Not one of you thought that I could be trusted with such information?"

There was nothing that I feared more than a furious aristocrat.

"It wasn't a question of trust. It was more a... Security."

Hamilton opened his mouth to protest, but was quickly shot down by Earnshaw, whose usual childlike and chipper voice had been changed beyond all recognition. He was as white as a sheet.

"But how? How did anyone find out?"

The crisis within his little team seemed to bring the best out in the Captain, who immediately sprang to his feet and returned to his usual pacing around the room and his strong booming voice responded.

"I have asked myself the same, Harry. But have come to the conclusion that it does not really matter. I don't much care for who let out our little secret, if anyone did at all. The fact of the matter is we are moving, we are going to Albert. And we must face the consequences of what will happen together, as a team. It does not matter who was told what and when, what matters is that we are all in this together. Is that understood?"

I was reassured somewhat by the strong, stern words from the Captain, and for a moment I found myself enjoying his little monologue, like it was something from Shakespeare. But I perhaps enjoyed it a little too much, as I found myself as the only one who was drawing the Captain's stares, the only one who had not yet responded to his question, that I had presumed was rhetorical.

"Yes, sir. Understood."

"Good. I'm glad that we are all on the same page. However, just because we are being moved this does not mean that any of us are off the hook. Especially you McKay, I'm sorry to say. The brass wanted you locked up and sent for a court-martial, but I petitioned them as much as I possibly could to make sure that you stayed with all of us. Unfortunately, the only way to keep all of us together was by moving as a team. The brass know that you are vital to the effectiveness of this team and have agreed to let you operate until the date of your court-martial. We will continue, together, until that day.

"We are not exactly in the Colonel's good books at the moment, gentlemen. So, we must do everything within our ability to make sure that we are as close to that book as we possibly can be. Agreed?"

This time, I was one of the first to respond.

"Right then, pack your things, we are moving out of here in the next hour. Say goodbye to Porky Paul if you have to. We will not be coming back."

I would say goodbye to him, as there was one thing that I needed him to do for me before I left.

I still hadn't quite got around to emptying that hip flask. Instead, I would need to refill it.

5

The room was incredibly silent, even the faint rumbling of artillery seemed to be drowned out by the melancholy and pessimism that was suffocating each one of us, as we got used to our new surroundings.

It was slightly fresher looking in our new billet than it had been at Porky Paul's, but it had none of the charm and draw to it that we had become used to. This was not our home, this was merely a room with some beds in it.

I swirled my hip flask around, trying to drum up any noise that I possibly could to fill the doom and gloom that each of us felt trapped with. There wasn't all that much left of it, and I burnt a hole in my pocket merely paying Porky Paul for a few drops of the stuff.

I had tried to ration as much of it as I possibly could, knowing full well that the chances of Earnshaw being able to work his magic in a new part of town so soon, would be virtually impossible. In fact, I don't think Earnshaw had muttered a single word for the whole journey to Albert, with very little coming from his mouth since.

Maybe it was for the best, I told myself. Maybe once I had run out, I would have to teach myself to never rely on it again and that there was a chance that I would slowly get used to not having it. In a way, I was looking forward to it, as it meant that I could become a fully functioning member of the human race once more. It felt like years since I had been without it, without having that dark, thick liquid by my side for me to fall back on the minute I felt uneasy.

But you need it to work. You are nothing without it.

"Give it a rest, will you? You're like a broken record. All you think about is your next drink."

I looked around me, as I always did now, just to doublecheck that no one else had heard it. His voice popped into my head more often recently, speaking to me so much that it felt like he was still alive. We had spoken more to each other in the three weeks since he had died, than we had done in the last two months of his life.

Bob Sargent's voice had lost the forceful and gruff characteristics to it that had defined him in the last few weeks of his life, and the genteel paternal-like tones that I had first heard had returned. It was almost like I was an eighteen-year-old soldier again, standing in the frontline fire bay nervously twitching around the trigger, with Bob standing by my side comforting me.

His voice, now a ghoulish echo around my head, had continued to comfort me in the last few weeks, but especially the last couple of days as we all wondered what lay in store for us. On more than one occasion, I felt like replying to him to ask his advice and to question why he had left me.

But it was that feeling of having him by my side that

made me feel insecure, like I was unable to mourn like the rest of the team. Maybe my denial in accepting his death was the very reason why I could not feel sad over the empty bed, that had screamed from the corner of the room above the *Café de Fleur.*

I needed urgently to stop thinking, as going round and round in this cycle of feeling sorry for myself was doing no one any favours at all. More importantly than that, I was the senior NCO of a group of men whose morale was so low that it wouldn't surprise me if I had found that each one of them had deserted by teatime.

It was the one piece of advice that Bob had given me that I had started to listen to. I needed to be their NCO, a man that they could go to with all their problems and feel like I was going to sort them out.

"You want a smoke, McKay?"

The young Scot continued to stare up at the ceiling, unblinking, his arms folded across his chest, his legs crossed at the ankles. He hadn't said a single word ever since the Captain had broken the news to us. He was avoiding absolutely any kind of human interaction, which was worrying me.

I began to question whether the Captain's judgement had been correct, and that persuading his superiors to let us all continue to operate was totally the wrong decision. How could any of us make a single rational decision when our heads were all over the place? Particularly McKay's.

I shook the carton of cigarettes under his nostrils, trying to waft the smell of un-used tobacco under his nose, to lull him out of the trance that he was in. There was no response, not even a shake of the head.

"Cards, then?"

Still, nothing. The more that I tried the more into himself I felt like McKay was becoming. I couldn't blame the poor fellow, I would have felt the same if I was in his situation.

As I stared at the blue and purple blotches all over his knuckles, I began to recall what had happened that had landed us all in so much trouble. McKay, in a moment of madness and weakness, had stolen British maps which he intended to plant in a German frontline trench. Not one of us had seen it coming, which meant that really, we all had to share a portion of the blame.

Not one of us had ever voiced concern over McKay since, or audibly expressed disbelief that a man was able to do such a thing, because deep down we all knew that each one of us were capable of such an act. It was something that continually played on my mind, especially now that Bob was gone.

I was distracted by a low and consistent scraping, as Hamilton continued to clean his rifle that he had clung to for our entire journey to Albert. It was almost soothing to me, but to Earnshaw it was a source of irritation.

"Do you really think you're going to live long enough to use that again?"

Hamilton looked up surprised, "Don't see why not. It pays to be prepared."

Earnshaw scoffed, "You don't get it do you? They're not going to let us get close enough to the enemy to ever use a weapon like that again. We are liabilities now, we're surplus to requirement. We'll be dead the minute we put our foot on the bottom of that ladder."

"You don't know that."

"Oh, I do. I really do."

"Earnshaw," I growled "that's not what is going to happen. We will be sent out on an operation, and we will carry it out to the best of our ability. You heard the Captain, he has petitioned the brass. They have agreed."

"See?" butted in Hamilton, quite unnecessarily, "there's a possibility that we will just be able to carry on as normal."

Hamilton did nothing except open himself up to an attack from Earnshaw.

"You really are a fool, aren't you? Nothing will carry on as normal now. Even if the brass do let us live to see the next operation, there is absolutely no way that we will live through it."

"How did you get to that?"

"Because, Hamilton, things are different here. The way the war is fought is different here. We don't know the land here, the terrain. It will not be the same as it was back near *Le Plantin*. It's made of different stuff, it reacts to artillery differently, it reacts to footsteps differently. Nothing will be the same again."

"And since when did you become an expert on French geography?" retorted Hamilton, "there is a chance that it's the same, we haven't moved all that far."

"Okay then," rebutted Earnshaw, setting himself up on the edge of the bed as if he was a barrister about to deliver his closing statement to the jury.

"It's not just the land. It's the enemy here. They are the same army, but different soldiers. We do not know where their strengths and their weaknesses are. Before we had that information. Now we do not.

"We do not know where their machine guns are. We

do not know where the sniper hideouts are, we do not know whether they have underground bunkers, or whether they stick their heads up every twenty minutes to say hello to the British.

"We have absolutely no idea what we are faced with. And now, we will have no time to evaluate the situation here. The brass will simply expect us to pick it up and become just as successful here as we were back in *Le Plantin*. But it doesn't work like that. That is weeks, if not months of hard work, of reconnaissance and observation simply watching the enemy. We will not have that luxury here. Got it?"

Hamilton got it. So did the rest of us. Earnshaw was right, there was very little that we could do now except for accept our fate. Earnshaw flopped back onto his bed in resignation and adopted a similar position to the one that McKay had frozen himself into. I felt like doing exactly the same.

Hamilton continued to scratch away at his rifle, stubbornly continuing to clean it in preparation for what might be asked of us. I admired his optimism, as deep down I knew that what Earnshaw said had some element of truth in it. It was unlikely that we were ever going to get close enough to the enemy to use our weapons ever again.

Besides, we were under the command of different men, who had had different experiences of war and different ideas of how to fight this one. It was possible that we would be used merely as bait for an advance, or used as nothing more than glorified infantrymen, who had a nice comfy bed compared to the rest of the men.

"Yeah... Well, I still think our lives are worth fighting

for. I don't think we should give up just yet." The optimism of the young British aristocrat was admirable, however stupid it made him look with the others. But I knew I had to side with him, as the Captain was all but useless in this situation.

It seemed like the whole debacle was eating him up more than it was eating McKay up. There was something deep within him that was troubling him far more than he was letting on. I got the distinct impression that he had not told us the whole truth. Which was something that, if all the others got wind of, could lead to a full meltdown of the entire team.

I just hoped that none of them could read the Captain as well as I could.

The question that continued to sit on my lips, but never tumble from them, was how McKay had been found out. How had they known?

It was the question that everyone wanted to know the answer to, but at the same time eternally fearful of hearing.

Earnshaw had grown incredibly pale at the revelation from Captain Arnold, and I thought for a moment that maybe the orderly who had cared for him in the hospital whilst injured, had become his confidant in the matter. Or maybe he had just overheard a sleep talking Harry, as he mumbled his way through his memories.

But the guilt that was etched on Harry's face was not pure enough to indicate his implication in the matter.

McKay, even though he was ashamed of what he had done, was not stupid enough to have handed himself in. And Sergeant Hughes was already dead. For a moment, I even suspected myself but could not recall any conversation with anyone outside of this room about what had happened to McKay, which left only the Captain. And Bob.

It was a thought that I did not want to entertain, but it seemed like the most realistic option at the time. Bob had serious issues with the way that the team was being run, primarily with the way that their Sergeant seemed to be an alcoholic.

He was furious with the way that the Captain always wanted to back me up, even if that meant that I was allowed to bend the rules. Maybe, it was possible anyway, that he had seen no other way to get me kicked out of the group, than to see the whole team disbanded completely.

A war weary and efficient Sergeant with a slight drink problem was not a serious enough charge to get us all dispersed, but treachery and desertion certainly was.

For the first time since he had died, I wondered to myself that maybe Bob had been the one that had gone above the Captain's head.

It was even possible that Bob had got himself killed deliberately.

6

The atmosphere gradually eased over the next few days, as we milled around the town of Albert, pleased as punch that we hadn't yet been killed as a punishment for what we had done.

Slowly, each one of us had come out of our shells, all of us apart from McKay that was. But we had taken a few tentative steps outside, and familiarised ourselves with the small town that we were now forced to call home.

The others spent many hours doing whatever it was that took their fancy when we were in a town such as Albert, with Earnshaw even managing to make a few promising contacts that had promised to fill up my hip flask at the earliest opportunity. Which was brilliant news for me as I had had a seventy-two-hour headache, that had plunged me into an awful mood with everyone.

I had spent many hours staring at the ruins of the local basilica, which had become something of target practice for the German artillery. The large cathedral type building enthralled me, not least for the way that it's high, imposing tower somehow remained relatively intact, despite the rest of the building laying like crumbs all around it.

The thing that I marvelled at the most, was the golden statue that lent at the most precarious of angles from the top of the tower.

"The golden virgin," a passing soldier had announced to me one morning, "it was knocked from its pedestal a few months ago now. The war won't end until that statue falls to the ground. You mark my words."

He had wandered off with a smirk, but it was a remark that I, for some reason, took very seriously. The statue itself seemed to hang at almost a ninety-degree angle, the Madonna holding out a golden baby back towards the rest of the town. It seemed almost impossible for it to stay in position, unless it had been held in by some supernatural power.

For a moment, I found myself almost believing the passing Tommy's remark.

As I spent hour after hour, day after day, wondering around the small little town, I eventually realised that it wasn't just McKay who was facing the possibility of a firing squad, but all of us, the truth that probably should have dawned on me far quicker than it had done.

We had all, with the exception of Hamilton, entered into a secret agreement that amounted to nothing short of treason, the one crime that seemed to carry more of a fear to it than desertion. It had led to many hours of questioning myself, asking what I could have done better to uphold the secret just a little while longer.

As I stared at the small golden head of the baby

which had once stood atop the basilica, I always found myself coming to the same conclusion.

You always knew you were going to die. Why does it matter how it happens?

At that point, I would always turn on my heel and walk down the main street which, if you walked in the wrong direction would take you all the way to the frontline.

We all spent as much time as we possibly could out in the town of Albert, as it helped us to distract from all the unanswered questions that floated around our tiny little room. It was only the Captain who refused to venture on a sightseeing tour of the town itself.

One unanswered question, however, was eventually answered after a little over a week of milling around Albert making a nuisance of ourselves, whilst also trying to forget the predicament that we found ourselves in.

"Snipers!" announced the odd Captain, unnecessarily loudly for the small room that we were in, but none-theless succeeding in grabbing all of our attention. He was a tall, wiry man, with an overly punch-able face, which I soon put down to the bad mood that I was in.

His jawline was strong and defined, but his lower jaw seemed to poke out further than the rest of his face, giving him the aura of a horse. His eyes were energetic and bright, a result of the innocence that he had retained for not seeing the same things that we had done. I tried to give him the benefit of the doubt, and reasoned that maybe it wasn't out of his own choice that he was in a relatively safe command.

This Captain, Gilman I thought he had called himself, was the officer in charge of counter sniper measures in the area. Gilman was convinced that the German sharpshooters in the sector had upped their game in recent weeks, but had been waiting for a team of men to be placed at his disposal. It seemed as if the senior officers in this sector knew that whoever was going to deal with this captain's problems, were going to end up dead very quickly. Which seemed to suit us down to the ground.

"The German sharpshooters are better than anything that we have at this moment in time, gentlemen. Unfortunately, I do not think we will be up to their standard for a very long time. Which means that, rather than simply copying their methods, we need to tackle the problem head on. Which means I need you men.

"The sharpshooters around here seem to have free rein wherever they go. They can occupy any part of the German frontline that they want, and they seem to skulk around No Man's Land as if it was Hyde Park. As a result, these snipers are now killing our lads as if it is some sort of an abattoir. It has fallen on my shoulders to at least try and stem the flow of blood that gushes in this sector every day."

He inspected each and every one of us as his eyes slowly panned their way around the room. For a moment it looked like he was staring straight into our souls as if he was suspecting us of being one of the German snipers ourselves. In actual fact, it was probably more likely that he was bewildered that the stinking men who sat before him were even actually up to the task.

I wondered if anyone had told him why we had suddenly appeared in Albert. If he knew the truth, I wondered if he'd still be standing there at all.

"As far as we are aware, the Germans are way ahead of us in terms of sniper tactics and the weapons that they have. It is my belief that some of the sharpshooters in this sector have a new rifle, one which we are very keen to take a look at. I also believe that they have developed a new type of optic sight, one which is far superior to our own."

"Everything else that they seem to have seem to be better than ours," bemoaned Earnshaw dejectedly. Everyone ignored his comment.

"You say you believe," I queried, "is this not a widely held belief?"

The Captain mulled over what I had to say, before his nose turned upwards as if he had detected a foul smell. I did not take it personally.

"No, Sergeant. I'm afraid that it isn't. Unfortunately, it is only me and my men that I have on the ground that believe this to be true. No one else higher up than me seems to believe that the Germans are possible of having better technology than us. Which is why I have had to wait so long for some resources to explore the possibility."

"So, what is it that is to be our task, Captain?" piped up Captain Arnold, who had remained unnaturally silent in the corner of the room.

"Well, it would be jolly good of you to help us all out. Ideally, I would like your help in trying to obtain one of the German rifles, complete with these new sights that I have been telling you about. I know that it sounds almost quite ridiculous to ask, but I am led to believe that if anyone is able to do it, it will be you chaps."

None of us even looked at each other in bewilderment now, as nothing seemed able to surprise us anymore. Ever since that we had been together, we had been asked to do the most ridiculous tasks that could ever be dreamt up. And this one certainly seemed to be up there with the worst ones to try and get us killed.

"That's going to be one devil of a job, Captain," snorted Captain Arnold. "How on earth are we going to be in the right place at the right time to try and bag ourselves one of those?"

"Well," smirked Gilman, as if he had been waiting for that question all afternoon, "there is one sharpshooter in particular that we have our eye on. He is perhaps one of the best. He routinely takes out our men, even if they have their head above the parapet for half a second. But he is a slave to habit, he always seems to snipe in the same area, at roughly the same time, but with a lethal accuracy. We have developed a plan that, with your help, will help us to take this man out and to retrieve his rifle. I will not pretend that it will be easy, but it will save many lives."

"But let me guess," chimed in Earnshaw, "it will more than likely end up in us lot being dead?"

To his credit Captain Gilman didn't dance around the subject.

"Yes. Most likely. It is entirely possible that you will all end up dead. But this is war, isn't it?"

His smirking face suddenly became even more punch-able.

7

"Sergeant William Lawrence, pleased to meet you."

I looked the man up and down for a few moments, trying to work out what kind of a bloke he really was. He was a young chap, the brightness of his skin told me as much, but the rest of his face already gave away that he had had a hard life. His head seemed to sit almost crookedly on his neck, which in turn sat at an awkward angle on top of the shoulders, making him look like an almost comical sculpture that had been chiselled whilst its maker was half drunk.

His shoulders seemed to be pushed as far forward as they would possibly go and his arms hung around his waist, as if he had no control over them whatsoever. The way that he held himself made him look like he was more like an animal than a human being. The awkward measurements of his body were highlighted even further when he sat down, where his right arm appeared far longer than the left. Maybe it was. Maybe it was that that made him so good at his job.

The most bewildering feature of all was the bumpy and uneven scar that ran along the length of his cheekbone, as if he had once upon a time had a replacement bone inserted underneath it. I made a quick note to find out what had caused that.

"And you?" interrogated the Captain quite aggressively.

"Lance Corporal Harold Chester, Sir." The younger looking man was in complete contrast to Lawrence, his fresh skin was smooth and appeared as if it had been pulled tightly, so that there were no wrinkles whatsoever. He stood up straight with his shoulders pushed so far back it looked almost as if he was pushing his head further forward. Based on his posture alone, I quite easily could have mistaken him for Hamilton from behind. From afar they could have even been cousins.

"You're not British, are you?" mumbled Earnshaw.

"So, you're the clever one of the bunch, then?" smirked Sergeant Lawrence. He ended his sentence with an upward inflection, as if he was going to continue on saying something, which made the silence even more awkward than it already was.

"Depends on your definition of British," interjected Chester, as he shot a sideways glance to his Sergeant.

Earnshaw opened his mouth to speak, but then slowly closed it again to avoid making himself look like a fool in front of our two newcomers. To his relief Sergeant Lawrence spoke up.

"We are Canadians," he announced proudly. "I'm from Ontario, Chester here is from Québec."

"I have family in Ontario," bumbled Hamilton, "whereabouts are you from?"

Lawrence seem to shuffle around on his feet, full of nerves for a moment, before he finally found the confidence to speak.

"Berlin."

"Say that again?"

"Many settlers in my town had German ancestry, so they named it Berlin. It is not exactly the best place to be living in, I know. There's a lot of anti-Germanness there right now."

"Unbelievable," muttered Earnshaw, "why don't they change the name?"

"As I said, a lot of settlers were from Germany. Some of them are still proud of their heritage."

"And you? Do you have German blood in you?"

"What did you say your name was again?"

"Earnshaw."

"You don't half ask a lot of questions, do you?"

Earnshaw's unanswered question clearly burned a hole in his conscience, but he swallowed his pride and kept quiet for the time being.

Chester turned around for half a second, making sure that the door that he had just walked through was still there, and when Lawrence noticed he gave him a quick dig in the ribs. He quickly turned to face us once again.

"So, you're the lads that can help us ping our sniper, are you?"

"Apparently so," I answered.

"I tried to tell the Captain I don't think I really need you, but he wouldn't listen. All I need is half a second of seeing that pig and I'll put a bullet in between his eyes."

Lawrence was incredibly matter-of-fact about the whole situation, to the point where his face suddenly reddened at the thought of the local sniper. I wondered if he'd had some sort of dealings with him before.

"You find it easy then, all this?"

It was the first time that McKay had spoken in days and, for a moment, his voice sounded more alien than the two Canadian voices that I had recently discovered. "All this killing, you are comfortable with it?"

Lawrence looked puzzled for a moment as if asking such a question in the middle of a war like this was the most bewildering thing that he had ever heard. But then he noticed McKay was serious and that his question was not rhetorical.

"Yeah, I do find it easy. They started it, dragged me a few thousand miles away from my home and are now killing my friends. So yeah, it is easy."

Chester began to scratch at something on the back of his neck, and I suddenly got the impression that he didn't feel quite the same way as his Sergeant it did. Lawrence was indifferent to what he was doing and matter of fact, but Chester looked quieter, methodical. As if he thought through the moral implications of absolutely everything that he did, before he carried it out. A man such as that could not have a clear conscience in a war like this one.

Lawrence read the startled look on McKay's face, and reasoned with himself that he had to justify what he was doing as a valued part of the war.

"Look, this is a war. Men die. I thought you lot would have known that more than anyone. At the end of the day we're not all that different to you. You get up nice and personal with them, then slot them. We just do it from a little bit of distance. Same war, different way of fighting it. That's all it is."

His little speech was quite definitive, and no one dared to carry on in the same topic. For a little moment, there was silence, which we all took as an opportunity to spend in the company of ourselves.

I suddenly began to recall the poor man who had been a victim of a German sharpshooter a couple of weeks before. I had watched him die, I had wanted him to die, as his incessant calling out for anyone who might listen had begun to grind my exhausted conscience.

His throat had been ripped open by a round, as if a pair of fleshy curtains had been pulled back to expose the poor man's windpipe and the tidal wave of blood that had come with it. The man had been a total mess of flesh and blood, but still he had continued to look at me with his youthful, optimistic eyes. It was something that I would never forget.

I wondered if, had he survived a little bit longer, that he would still be staring blankly now, in some hospital bed somewhere as he slowly recovered. I had never been as close to death as that man had been, but I couldn't think of what was going through his mind as he stared up at the exhausted Sergeant who was trying to help him. Maybe he was seeing his father as he looked at me, which gave me hope that I would see my own family as I gave up my life.

Slowly, the boy's face and glare faded from my mind and I began to tune myself back into the room that I was sat in, and the conversation that flowed around without me.

"Look, we didn't choose to go to war. You Brits did that for us. We didn't really have much of a choice, but I volunteered anyway. A lot of lads my way were joining so

I thought I'd go with them. Turns out I'm quite good at all this killing malarkey after all."

The more that he spoke, the easier I was finding it to listen to him, the long rolling sounds of his voice making me imagine it whispering through valleys and across unending fields. It was almost acting like some sort of calming influence on me.

"What about you?" asked Earnshaw, "How have you ended up here?"

"I had a bit of a different life to Sergeant Lawrence. I was off to college, my father was paying for my education, a good one too. But then, something got in the way and it was all called off. At least it was in my eyes. Next best thing was the army. That was just before this party started."

Hamilton suddenly became very interested in Chester, sliding his chair across the floor so that it was closer to him.

"You had a falling out with your father?"

"Of sorts, yeah."

"Me too..." he said dreamily, "Me too."

"Mind if I asked what happened?"

Hamilton appeared almost delighted that someone was showing an interest and launched immediately into a long-winded story of childlike intrigue and naivety, which led him all the way to the British Army.

"My father doesn't even know that I joined up. Although, having said that, he has some friends in very high places. So high they'd give you a nose bleed."

We were all suddenly very keen to hear Hamilton's story, but we allowed Chester to carry on the conversation.

"How high up are we talking?"

"My father, he works in the Admiralty. So, quite high up I suppose."

"What...and you came here, when you could have had a lovely job there? All over a disagreement about how to live your life?"

The Canadian Sergeant was incensed.

"Yes. I suppose I did. Quite funny really, if you think about it."

"You've got a skewed definition of funny, buddy."

We shared a few more silent cigarettes, before convening around a grotty looking table to play a card game that even McKay didn't know how to play. Although that never stopped him from winning one or two rounds.

"So, tell me," I asked as I lit a full complement of cigarettes, "Why is it that they have sent two of you? That makes our job harder, to keep you both alive. And surely it makes it more likely that you two will be spotted, doesn't it? Why risk the other man's life."

Lawrence took a few over-exaggerated puffs on his cigarette, giving it a look of disdain in between drags, before inconveniencing himself by delivering an answer.

"Because, Tommy Atkins, we like to work in pairs. It can get awful lonely sitting out there hour after hour with no one to even share the air around you with."

He finished his answer there and offered no indication that he was to carry on.

"That's the only reason that we have to take the two of you? Blimey, if I'd known that then I would have brought my cat for you, to keep you company," Earnshaw spat as he struggled to keep his cigarette in his mouth.

"That's one reason," Chester suddenly babbled, "the other is to confirm the kill."

"You mean you're so blind you can't even work out if you hit what you were aiming at?"

"No, you stupid Red Coat," Sergeant Lawrence withdrew his smoke from his mouth, "Otherwise we could simply announce that we had hit the Kaiser and we could all go home."

"Oh, that makes sense."

"I'm glad it wasn't too difficult for you."

A few more hours of cards and cigarettes ensued, before the night began to morph into the early hours of the morning.

"Right then, I suppose that's us for the night, boys."

We bade farewell until the next time we saw them, which we would spend much more constructively going over maps and alternative plans for when the first one inevitably nose-dived.

As each of us began our routine to shut down for the night, I caught Hamilton out in the hallway.

I gripped his arm, as if accosting him for a crime.

"Hamilton. Your father. I reckon a well-timed letter of reconciliation might just save McKay's skin. What do you reckon?"

He chewed it over for a moment, silently, as if it was a tough bit of beef.

"I'm not sure, Sarge. He was pretty mad the last time that I saw him. In fact, it might make matters even worse."

"He's your father Hamilton. I know you don't think this will affect you, but the top brass taking the Court Martial won't know that you didn't know until recently, will they? They'll assume you're just as guilty as the rest of us."

I wasn't sure if I was getting through to him, but the mild blackmail was all that I had left in my arsenal of persuasion.

He tussled with the chewy bit of beef in his mouth once again as he gave it some consideration. I did the same.

I wondered why I had done it for a moment, my initial reaction being one of pride at spotting an opportunity and gripping it with both hands. But soon after, I was overcome with a guilt that I had not taken the initiative to preserve McKay, but to ensure that I myself had a future.

It wasn't something that was sitting as easily with me as I would have hoped.

"I'll give it some thought, Sergeant."

"Okay. But whatever you decide, do it sharpish. We don't have long before we leave. And I don't know if you'll be alive this time next week. Okay?"

"Yes, Sergeant."

8

I stared at Hamilton for quite some time, taking in every single one of his features, as if that would act as some sort of persuasion to get the man to write the all-important letter. I wondered how much his father would actually be able to help, if at all, and whether or not I had been fair on him by putting such a large weight upon his shoulders.

Life was tough on us all, but the thought that I had piled something else onto Hamilton's plate, that may do more harm than good, made me feel infinitely worse.

His mouth seemed to be permanently pursed, as if he was sucking on a particularly bitter lemon, and I thought that maybe it was as a result of the falling out with his father that had left his face in the state that it was in. Hamilton always seemed to scowl at everyone, not because he was annoyed with them or distrusted them, but because that was simply how his face was.

There was something rather distinct missing from his persona, something that absolutely everyone else had, but which he managed to repel consistently. The cigarette smoke clung to the outer edges of the room and I began to reason that maybe that was why the walls in Porky Paul's establishment were rancid and flaking. I wondered how long it would take us to render these walls in a similar condition.

Hamilton still refused to smoke, something which I had been rather determined to maintain when I had first been sent to France. I admired him for his determination and willpower, but at the same time couldn't quite understand his reasons for refraining. What I found even more perplexing was the fact that he did not drink. Not even a drop.

As a result, apart from the Captain, he was the only one that I felt comfortable offering the hip flask to.

I began to look around the other faces, for a change, and so that Hamilton didn't pick up on the wilful glare that was burning into the side of his face.

I panned the room, interrupted by a wide, all-encompassing figure filling my vision.

"Andrew, could I have a word?"

Captain Arnold spoke before I could even have the chance to look up at him. He had always been like that, incredibly impatient, to the point where he would stop people from finishing their sentences, as he already had the gist of what they were trying to say. More recently, however, he had refrained from interrupting people, instead using the surplus time to lock himself away in the deepest chambers of his own consciousness, deliberating what he would do or say next.

He continued to carry around the leather-bound notebook, a present from Earnshaw, frequently found in between his thumb and forefinger, eagerly anticipating what it was that would be scrawled across its pages next. I suddenly had a burning desire to read what was inside.

"Of course, Sir."

As I followed him from the occupied room and down the stairs, I noticed that he had started to move considerably slower than when I had first encountered him. Before, there had always been a vibrant air of enthusiasm and optimism about him, which was now seemingly being overtaken by what appeared to be the characteristics of an old man.

He gingerly stepped down the staircase, side on, as if he had a dodgy knee or two, and he sighed deeply instead of gently releasing his breath.

The premature aging extended too to his ability to sleep. Many nights I had awoken to see that his gas desk lamp was still hissing away aggressively, the sound of which was drowned out by his occasional deep exhales.

I never intruded on what he was doing, and I certainly never enquired as to what was keeping him up all those hours, but simply fell back on the assumption that it was something above my station.

Something was keeping him up though, and it was my job to find out what. It was beginning to worry me. It could quite likely end up in getting me killed if he wasn't too careful.

≈

I WAS surprised at how brilliant the dying sun was, as it lit up the whole sky above me in the most fabulous shade of orange that I had ever seen in my life. I let the water gush to my eyes for a moment, as I marvelled in its beauty, before I could bear the pain no longer and was forced to turn my face away from the source.

Captain Arnold turned to face me, his features a mere silhouette against the dipping sunlight. I was glad, as I knew that I wouldn't be subjected to his forlorn, drooping face that had adorned our commanding officer for the last week or so now.

"Andrew, I..." his voice trailed off and he turned his face away and began walking down the street. Somewhere, far off in the distance, a trio of artillery shells connected with the solid structure of the earth. Even from the distance that we were from them, we could still feel the tremors. Another constant reminder of this war.

There was something weighing heavy on his conscience, the kind that weighs a man down so heavily that his shoulders begin to curl forwards every time he considers it. It was eating away at his insides, and he was using me as his sounding board, he needed me to get it off his chest.

Say something.

I hated the expectation of it all, the silent demands for me to come up with something heartfelt and meaningful, to make the Captain suddenly feel ten tonnes lighter. Even though I knew it could end up saving my life, nothing but the most superficial, and futile words, would tumble from my mouth.

Something. Anything.

"It will be okay, Sir. We have been on far more difficult tasks than this one and come back unscathed."

Silently, he acknowledged my existence with a slight nod of the head, before continuing to potter down the road, quite aimlessly. I wondered how much further he would walk, and if I wasn't to stop him soon, then there was a possibility that he would walk all the way back to Blighty if he could.

"You know that we're good, Terence. There aren't any other men that are up to the task. They're resilient. They're raring to get going again."

He stopped, clicking his feet to a halt in the most perfect of parade square drill. He scoffed and for a second, I felt quite offended.

"It's not that," he started, before allowing the croak at the back of his throat to get the better of him once more. I turned my face away from him, quite urgently, as I convinced myself that if I was to look at him much longer, then I would see large, aristocratic tears streaming down his face. And I didn't want to see my commanding officer and friend reduced to that.

Besides, I had no idea how I was meant to react to something like that.

"I can—"

I felt like forcing his shoulders round so that he was facing me and giving him a cracking great slap across his cheek.

Spit it out! Why can't you speak?

At this rate, we were going to be there all night. Which worried me, as I needed my sleep.

"What is it, Sir? Terence?" I tried to coax him out of his shell, as best I could. I started to feel like a parent who was forcing their child to go and make some friends.

Finally, he found the courage to complete an entire sentence. I felt like giving him a round of applause.

"It's not that, Andrew. It's about McKay."

He began to lower his tone as a horse and cart, that looked far too battered and abused to still be carrying weight, trundled past us, hitting every groove and divot in the road that was possible. We nodded back to the French soldier perched in the cart, but the Captain stared the man down until he was at least half a mile away.

He didn't want a soul to hear what it was that he was about to say.

"McKay. It's been troubling me," his eyes suddenly flashed a brighter hue than the normal hazelnut that I was used to, as if something had possessed him to say what was on his mind.

"I have been giving it all a great deal of thought. The court martial, you know."

Of course, I knew.

"Well, I...What with this latest job we've been given. And, you must understand that I do feel tremendously guilty about the whole affair..."

Another horse and cart approached, this time laden with boxes of ammunition as it made its way to the front. The same staring protocol was applied.

"I was thinking, and the thought suddenly popped into my head that maybe it would be best if McKay was to get himself killed tomorrow night."

I thought I had misheard, but the Captain was attentive enough to repeat himself. His eyes seemed to flash again, as if he wasn't quite believing what was coming from his mouth. This ran deeper than just a brief thought in the early hours of the morning.

It was the first time that I had started to lose my trust in Captain Arnold.

"I thought that maybe if he was killed, it would make

the whole thing a lot easier. For McKay, for us, for everyone. If he was to die, then there would be no court
martial, his family wouldn't have to go through whatever
happens to him for one thing. If he was found guilty his
whole village would know in no time."

I felt like stumbling around on my feet for a second,
as if I had just been dealt the most horrific blow to the
face that a boxer could ever deliver.

"But, Sir, there's still the question of the charges
against us. We conspired with McKay, remember."

The Captain, as ever, was resolute in the direction
that he wanted the conversation to go.

"But just say, hypothetically I mean, if McKay was to
be killed, would it be better for all of us?"

"I wouldn't be able to say, Sir."

It felt odd to address the Captain by his Christian
name in a situation such as this, and I found myself
wanting to distance my association from him in any way
that I could.

There were a few minutes of an uneasy, awkward
silence, as a group of Indian soldiers began to stumble
past us, offering up the weakest of salutes to the Captain
that I had ever seen in my life.

*Fair enough. It's not like he deserves a proper one right
now anyway.*

"There was a girl back at home, that I was due to be
married to. I was very fond of her and she of me. It was
one of those incredibly rare occurrences where the two
families were both very much in favour of a romantic
kind of love."

I wondered where he was going with the whole
conversation, and debated if he was suddenly going to

burst into tears, as he began to recall his life from before.

"But then, the Army came calling. And I put a halt on the whole thing. She has written since saying that she will wait until the war is all over, and that she will wait for me. But she believed that it would be over by Christmas, so who knows?"

He looked down at me with a smirk, "I don't think I'll be around too much longer. I don't think I ever will marry her. What do you think?"

I was too incensed to think at that moment in time, my only thoughts being filled of hallucinations of me knocking the Captain to the ground and screaming McKay's name as I did so.

"I made a sacrifice, Andrew. The girl or the army. The army won that one."

He cleared his throat and, as he stared across at the now non-existent sunshine, I could see him begin to sweep away the initial dampness of tears from his eyes.

"McKay has been fortunate," he went on. "He has been very fortunate. In fact, I think he's the only one that hasn't taken a hit so far…"

Maybe tomorrow his luck will run out.

The Captain didn't need to utter the words to regret them. He swallowed them up and left only a few indecipherable grunts in their place.

"That's because he's the best out of the lot of us," I jumped in, rather too forcefully.

I had no idea what was going through Captain Arnold's head, but the never-ending sentences and stories of sacrifice had started to make it sound as though that he was ordering me to get one of my men killed deliberately. And not just any old man, McKay was my best friend.

I had already got one of my best friend's killed in this war. I was certain that I would not let it happen again.

But there was something off about Captain Arnold after that, as if he still hadn't quite relieved himself of the almighty weight that was crushing down on his chest.

9

"Are you sure you are up to this?"

Bob's voice was back in my conscience again, this time faceless and bodyless. But still very much there, none-theless.

"Last time you went out, you got me killed. I'm not so certain that you will be able to keep young McKay alive. What makes you think that you can? The Captain has all but decided that he should die. It would be the best for the team. Isn't that what you said about me?"

GRHMN.

A swift slurp at the hip flask would silence him for now, as well as steadying the tremoring hand, that had more or less become a permanent feature of the dishev-elled man that I had become. For the first time in a long time, I stopped thinking about what the other men around me looked like, and started to focus on how I appeared to them.

I quickly put a stop to that, as I scared even myself.

I knew that most of them lived with the knowledge of

my hip flask and the quivering muscles that seemed to plague my every waking hour. I wondered for a moment if I really was their Sergeant, or if I was merely a glorified hospital patient, the men that surrounded me my nurses and orderlies.

Even if I wasn't hospitalised, I certainly convinced myself that these men were the ones looking after me, not the other way around.

Another quick sip. That should do the trick.

It did. Bob was gone, for now.

"You okay, Ellis?"

I looked back at the grinning Canadian.

"Fine, thank you, Lawrence."

He looked down at the hip flask, "Want to talk about it?"

"Not unless you want to talk about that scar of yours."

He rubbed away at the uneven scar across his cheek, the one that looked as if he had been struck by a ferocious lion.

"No chance. Even if I told you, you probably wouldn't believe me."

"I've lived the unbelievable, mate."

"That's a very good point."

He tapped the end of his nose and gave me a wink. "Maybe when we get back, Ellis."

If we get back.

"Last time you went out, you got me killed."

Bob's voice slowly morphed into a more drooling, soothing tone. It was slightly rough around the edges and it took me a while to realise that it was in fact Sergeant Lawrence's voice that now filled my mind.

"We have our own path out there, chaps. It's an observation post that we have used many times before. In a shell hole."

"Not just any shell hole," interrupted Carter, "it's covered and concealed quite well. Sheets of iron, bits of concrete and brick. Anything really to give us some cover while we're out there."

"We can move about relatively safely once we're in there," continued Sergeant Lawrence, "but it might get a bit cosy with you lot in there as well."

"Is there a more suitable option? For Hamilton, I mean," asked Earnshaw with a wry smile.

"Oh yes. How silly of me to forget," replied Lawrence, "for the sons of parliamentarians and the landed gentry, you'll find more room a hundred yards straight ahead of you. In the Bosche frontline. Seeing as it was your sort that sent us here."

Hamilton took the joke well, allowing the Canadian to slap him heartily on the back with an accompanying chuckle. The Captain on the other hand, chose to ignore him.

"We'll hole up there until just before sunrise. That should be around the same time as our little sharp-shooter friend begins to rear his head."

Lawrence began to stroke his rifle quite affectionately and I had noticed he did it as some sort of superstition. The stroking had increased, particularly over the last few hours, up to the point where he was doing it almost continuously, and the thought of doing something else was more of an inconvenience to him.

Even when he wasn't stroking his rifle, he seemed to be searching for it, never taking his gaze off it for too long, in case it went for a walk of its own accord or in case someone was to turn it on him themselves. It appeared to be a mythical superstition, almost like the hip flask in my breast pocket. Maybe Sergeant Lawrence and I weren't all that different after all.

"Right then," announced the Captain, trying to reassert some of his authority amongst the Canadians, who seemed to show no respect for him whatsoever. "Everyone collect what you need. You have fifteen minutes. Fifteen minutes."

His speech was short and deliberately curtailed, as if he was avoiding being in the limelight for now. Maybe he was. If I had just revealed to someone else that a member of my team would be better off dead, then there was no way that I could look myself in the eye, never mind let everyone else look up to me. He was a disgrace.

He is still your Captain. He still needs you, Andrew.

"You lot squeezed everything out? You better make sure that you have."

"Eh?"

Lawrence began to chuckle and allowed his compatriot to untangle the riddle.

"The latrines...you used them?" explained Chester, his soft tones, more reminiscent of a vicar than a soldier, rolled around the room, almost as much as his eyes did. "He likes that one, it's one of his favourites."

"It is," agreed Lawrence, a cigarette now bobbing around in his lips so much that it looked as though it would fall out at any moment.

"We can't have you lot fidgeting around too much once we get out there. We need to limit our movement. Use the toilet now and make sure you don't need to go later. The Germans, and the Brits for that matter, pretty much have the whole area that we'll be in zeroed. If they see any movement at all, we'll be flatter than a bank note. It gets pretty dangerous out there."

"Oi, you don't need to tell us that, chum. We've been out in No Man's Land as much as you have been," Earnshaw accusingly wagged a finger across at Chester, the easier target of the two.

"Oh, I doubt that very much, son," said Lawrence, stepping in to help his defenceless comrade. "Besides, from what I've heard, you like to do a bit of work and then shy away from it all for a couple of months."

Everyone spat as they descended into fits of laughter, even McKay could not restrain himself from having a little chuckle.

"It was six weeks!" screamed Earnshaw, "I was wounded, I nearly died!"

His protests drew nothing more than exaggerated guffaws, as the men who faced death drew happiness from anything they could latch onto. Seeing the situation was pointless, Earnshaw surrendered himself to the sneaking sniggers that loitered around the back of his throat. Once he got going, it seemed nothing would be able to stop him.

But No Man's Land was the perfect remedy for that.

～

I KEPT my body as flat as could be as I dragged my way under the nest of barbed wire that sat just inches above my head. If I caught myself on it at this early stage, then I was in for a very breezy journey into the darkness.

The trench ladder was placed on the fire step, an inch

perfect instruction issued by Chester who seemed to want to get everything absolutely right.

The two Canadians had been here before, there was no doubt about that, and they knew exactly how they wanted to proceed.

"Once we get up there, we're in charge, okay? This is our territory, our war. You got that?"

Captain Arnold was stunned into a silence that he could only agree to.

I felt millions of bits of dirt trying to worm their way down the front of my trousers, but I wriggled in earnest to prevent them from gaining entry. The hard, compact lumps of dirt that had formulated since the Canadian's last outing, began to dig into my stomach, like a child desperately seeking some kind of protection.

I waited there, as still as possible for a few moments, waiting for Chester to come up behind me and give me a tap. As I waited, I kept my head up, trying to glean any information that I could of our new terrain.

It was dangerous work, heading out into No Man's Land, and to do it blind, without even seeing the area in daylight, was particularly hazardous. I just felt blessed that we had two experienced men as our guides, and I hoped that we didn't slow them up so much that we all got the chop.

The countryside was in a perfect darkness, there was simply nothing from what I could see. There was not even a single darkened shadow that indicated the presence of a tree or some sort of building, not like I had expected to see No Man's Land populated by such things.

I was still none the wiser as to where the shell holes were, where the land rose and fell and where I would be able to grab a sip at the hip flask. I was completely blind. I even had a job to work out whether I was actually looking out at No Man's Land, or if it was just the bottom of Earnshaw's boot.

Eventually, I felt something prick the back of my leg. Then again.

Is he? Is he really? Yes! He's using his bayonet!

I recoiled aggressively as I sensed the sharpened tip of the bayonet move towards my leg for a third time, absolutely horrified that this time he might press a little too hard and draw blood. If he was to do that, then I would more than likely leap up and entangle myself in the British cobweb of barbed wire. I would be stranded.

I wondered if it was Chester's idea of a joke.

Our progress was slow and incredibly tiresome, the monotony of heaving oneself through a very shallow, hastily scraped ditch was not a pastime that I would be pursuing once this war was over.

The ditch itself was more as a guidance for the marksmen it seemed, as it offered no real protection whatsoever. All it would take would be a single flare, and the lot of us would appear like enlarged hedgehogs, wiggling their way through the night.

I prayed that none went up until we were safe.

I tried to control my breathing with every ounce of energy that I could spare, but the constant beads of sweat that cascaded down my body as I heaved, made matters even worse. I was shattered and I could feel Chester behind me getting impatient with our progress. I wondered if Lawrence, who was leading the pack, was feeling the same.

Come on. You're only twenty yards from your own frontline.

I needed a break, and soon, otherwise the pains and strains in my body were going to involuntarily manifest themselves as shrieks. For the time being, I continued on.

I tried to distract myself from the pain by thinking of other things. Of what might happen to us and what might possibly go wrong. But I soon put an end to all that once I had concluded that everything that could go wrong, would.

My mind was suddenly distracted by the voice of Bob Sargent once more, this time muttering something to himself in the back of my head.

Why are you there? How can I hear you?

I asked myself the same question over and over, as I repeated the same old actions to drag myself one yard closer to the sharpshooter's lair.

The more I experienced in this war, the worse I realised that I was becoming. I cared far less for myself and the men around me. I did not give any kind of consideration to the men on the end of my bayonet and even less to any family members that may actually miss them.

The tremors in my hands had become far more aggressive and frequent, to the point where I found it difficult to even light my own cigarette once they had taken hold. The only thing that could subdue them was a sip of the hip flask and even that was beginning to lose its effectiveness.

What was it? Fear? The paraffin? Remorse?

I couldn't pinpoint any of my feelings on one thing in

particular but started to formulate some sort of an answer in my own mind.

Maybe I was hearing Bob because I missed him. Or quite possibly it was something to do with the guilt. I had killed him, whichever way you looked at it. I was solely responsible.

The more I considered it, the more I realised that maybe the Captain's tale of sacrifice had not been so meaningless after all.

I needed to be released from the guilt that I was experiencing over the death of Bob; the death that was forcing me to the drink, to hear him and the never-ending tremors. And to do that, maybe I had to let myself simply leave this world to relieve my own conscience.

Maybe, just maybe, if McKay and I were to be killed tonight, I thought, then the rest of the team would be far better off for it.

10

Our pace was slow, and the sweat that dripped from every crevice of my body was copious by the time we made it to the sharpshooter's shell hole. The way that they had described it to us before, had made it sound almost like a luxurious room, but in actual fact was nothing more than a glorified hole that even a fox would have struggled to have slept in.

Nevertheless, it was reasonably comfortable for what it was, with a continuous roof above us and old shredded sacks beneath us, to try and keep us as dry as possible.

The two Canadians looked at home here and seemed almost frustrated that they had to share this space with us for the time being. It must have been nice for them to be able to have a small space that they could call their very own.

Chester began to work methodically, working his way through various checks and observations, that he clearly carried out each and every time he crawled out to the hole. Once he had finished everything that he needed to, he pushed his back up one of the sides of the hole and withdrew a small book from his pocket, which he immediately began to read as if none of us were anywhere near him.

I noticed that every now and then, he peered upwards from the pages, to doublecheck where Lawrence was and to make sure that there were no unwelcome additions to the shell hole. I got the impression that Lawrence was his good luck charm and that the constant looking over his shoulder had something to do with a previous experience, that these two men may or may not have shared.

All in all, the shell hole seemed reasonably well hidden and just as I found myself feeling quite comfortable in a small hole, Lawrence suddenly shifted himself around so that he was up at the front of the hole itself.

He began to gently push the corrugated iron sheet, that was our ceiling, which gave off only the faintest creak as he did so, but even that seemed loud enough to wake the dead out there. I looked around for a moment, quite alarmed, but then realised that Chester continued to read the pages of his book, and reasoned with myself that there was nothing to fear.

Coolly, calmly Lawrence began to pick up a deliberately placed rock and set it just underneath the sheet of iron, so that it propped one end open like a letterbox.

The slit that had opened up at one end of the shell hole was just about big enough for a rifle barrel to poke out from bravely, or a pair of binoculars to peer out from curiously. Being as dark as it was, there was not much point in doing either, but Lawrence duly began to manoeuvre himself, so that he was resting on the side of the hole, with his rifle up and ready for action.

The gap itself was not more than three or four inches high, but I began to entertain visions in my mind of a grenade or machine gun bullet zipping inside and tearing the flesh of all the poor souls who sat on the inside.

We were packed in so tightly, that I convinced myself that one, well placed round would be all that was needed to kill at least three of us.

But, I reasoned, these two had been here and done this before, and Chester who seemed to be the more nervous of the two, had no qualms in what Lawrence was doing and how he had done it. Therefore, I would just have to trust them, as they would have to trust me later on.

No one seemed to speak for what felt like hours but, when the silence was broken, it was by a barely audible whisper and for a moment it screamed even louder than my thoughts.

"We wait until morning now."

His voice was so timid and quiet that despite hearing every word, I was on the verge of asking for him to repeat himself.

"We'll take it in turns to keep watch. The rest of us will try and get some sleep. We've got a long night ahead."

"Sleep?" Earnshaw seemed to screech in the darkness.

"Now's as good a time as any. Besides, you're probably safer to sleep here than the frontline. You should be able to get a good night sleep."

"How do you work that one out?" Earnshaw, as all of

us, was not sold on the idea that Lawrence was trying to convince us with.

"Well, I've been doing it a while. And I'm still here, aren't I?"

There was no point in arguing with him, as what he had said was entirely true.

"I'll go first. Then Chester. And you lot can work it out between you who goes after that. I hope you lot know how to keep watch."

～

GENTLY, I unclamped my eyes, a sticky residue doing all that they could to keep them welded shut. For a few moments I let it have its way, but I knew that eventually the jostling pair of hands, that shook my shoulders from side to side, would win.

It was McKay, his face a picture of the stubbornness and worry that defined his life. His arms, far more powerful than any other man's that I had ever seen before, continued to pull me from side to side, despite the fact that my eyes were locked on to his.

I looked around. Everyone else was asleep. Whatever it was, it can't have been so urgent that he hadn't woken everyone else up as well.

"Your turn. On watch."

I breathed a sigh of relief, directly into McKay's face which he deflected with a swift waft of his hand. It was my turn to bear the weight of responsibility that everyone else had borne over the last few hours.

I slowly moved around, accidentally kicking the feet of the men who occupied the shell hole with me, as I manoeuvred my way around so that I could lie in the centre of the gap that Lawrence had opened up for us. McKay sidled up next to me.

"Use this," he breathed into my ear, as he fed a piece of cloth into my sweaty palms. "Chester gave it me. Place over the barrel of your rifle, helps keep us hidden."

As I settled in to my watch, I began to survey the scene before me, which must have taken me no more than twenty seconds. The early hours of the morning still clung to the debilitating lack of light, rendering me almost completely blind and robbing me of my most valuable sense. I could not even make out the higher sloping hill that I knew existed somewhere along here, that the Germans were able to watch from with ease.

Eventually, I began to feel McKay's breath on the back of my left hand, as he refused to rest and take his turn having a sleep. I looked across at him.

"Get some sleep, Fritz. You're going to need it."

He sighed, and breathed back in my direction, "I won't be able to sleep. I can't seem to switch off."

It was reasonable, and I was certain that I would have been exactly the same had I had a court-martial looming over my head as he did. I wondered what went on through his mind; whether he was concerned about his family finding out, the hearing itself or whether it was the sheer regret over what he had done that was keeping him up.

It must have been about three o'clock in the morning, the almost bizarre part of the night where nothing at all seems to stir, apart from two unstable and apprehensive trench raiders.

"What do you reckon about death?"

The words that came from his mouth took me by surprise and I almost waited for him to repeat himself, which didn't come. Instead, I turned to look at him and watched his small curious little eyes stare out over the non-existent landscape that screamed back at us.

"What?"

"When death comes. What do you think happens?"

"Well I... Well, I can't really say I'm entirely sure. Never really been there myself." I tried to turn the corners of my mouth into something to resemble a smile, but nothing came. "Why do you ask?"

He sat in silence for a few moments more, enjoying the darkness that seemed to cling to his skin. He ignored me for a couple of seconds, punctuating the silence with a few rustles from his clothing as it rubbed up against the dry sackcloth that littered the hole.

"I reckon that when you die, you're dead. There's nothing after that. I just hope that it's as painless as possible."

He had started to speak as if he had overheard the Captain, as if it was inevitable that, within a few hours, he would be dead.

There was nothing that I could do apart from simply stare at him and hope to heaven that he had no plans to take anyone else with him, wherever he was going.

Eventually, he sank back down into the hole and resembled something of a man who was trying his hardest to sleep. But I knew that he wasn't. A man with questions like that would never be able to sleep that easily.

Every now and then, a flare lit up the night sky, an opportunity that I took to look around me. The quivering light, tremoring so violently it looked as if it needed a drink as badly as I did, made it near on impossible for me to locate anything of any real importance. The flares arose almost dead ahead of me, which made looking in the direction of the German frontline a blinding task.

After a while, I taught myself that it was probably best to simply allow the flares to hiss in the night sky, before they threw themselves at the ground, letting the darkness close around me once more.

"Wake up, Andrew. You're going to get everyone killed, like you got me killed."

Bob's voice alerted me, my body jolting awake and for a moment I convinced myself that I had been sleeping. But in reality, I knew that I hadn't, and it was merely my body's way of telling me to keep as alert as possible.

"Andrew, listen to me. I am trying to help you, why won't you let me?"

I looked at the backs of my hands, expecting to see a violent tremble, at least in my little finger. But nothing was there, they were as steady as the rock that propped the corrugated iron open.

See? You don't need a drink.

"If you won't listen to me, maybe you'll listen to *that.*"

For a moment, I wondered what Bob was trying to tell me, but his voice slowly faded into nothingness, made far more prominent by the fact that there was a new noise in tow.

I continued to try and push Bob away and out of my mind, convinced that it was him who was playing tricks on me. I willed myself to stop hearing the noises that were crunching their way through my mind, before coming to the realisation that the dead could not fabricate noises out in No Man's Land. Especially ones that McKay could hear to.

He propped himself up on his forearms, his head tilted towards me but more so that he could get his ear closer to the noise, rather than to get a better look at me.

There was a scraping coming from somewhere ahead of us, a rhythmic almost methodical scratching noise, followed by a slight and delicate crunch.

I locked eyes with McKay.

It was a noise that we had heard before, it was one that we had created ourselves before. I was convinced that the Germans had heard the same noise when we were approaching.

It was the sound of a group of boots, as they slowly made their way across No Man's Land.

11

As I lay there, my fingers beginning to quiver expectantly, I listened intently to the footsteps that were approaching. I listened so hard to the noise that they were creating, that I began to imagine the heel to toe movement as they softly crunched their way through the debris and dirt that made up No Man's Land.

From where I was, I could not quite make out how far away they were, but there was one fact that was irrefutable. They were getting closer.

As ever, whenever I heard the crack of footsteps, I tried my utmost to estimate how many pairs of feet were making their way in my direction. And as always, I failed miserably in my task. There was simply no way of knowing how many men were staggering their way towards us, as one footstep interrupted another, each and every time that I focused in on it.

I began to rack my brains and try to recall a meagre piece of information that would enlighten me as to who the feet belonged to. I could not remember anyone mentioning the fact that there was a British patrol out tonight, there was no mention of a rewiring party and there was certainly no planned rendezvous with anyone else involved in our little operation.

As far as I was concerned, as the one on watch, I was treating these footsteps as hostile. As soon as I saw an associating figure, I would be squeezing the trigger with a fearless efficiency.

The noise continued to intensify, and for a moment I persuaded myself to move my head over to one side, so that my left ear could absorb all of the noise that was being made. I listened to it for a while and let my ear digest the vibrations that reached it.

The scraping noise was coming from dead ahead, which meant that, if they were to continue on the same course, it wouldn't be too long before they tripped over the corrugated iron that stuck up from the ground like a curious hare.

I knew that I needed to alert the others as to what was happening, but the thought suddenly crossed my mind that it wasn't totally impossible that it was simply another sniper team setting up for the night. It wouldn't have surprised me if the officers had failed to divulge all of the information of the night's events. We simply could not be trusted with that kind of thing.

But, if it was another sharpshooter patrol, I hoped desperately that they would assume the same of us if we had made any noise, otherwise it was feasible that both patrols could end up wiped out by one another.

I decided that it would be best to err on the side of caution, and so set about slowly moving my rifle from its resting position to a point where I knew that I could stare down the sights and out into the darkness. There was no point in rechecking to see if it was ready, as I knew I could just about trust myself to have made sure earlier on. When I pulled that trigger, my rifle would go bang.

Although I was certain that McKay could hear the noise, I buried one of my knees in his side several times over, to make sure that I had his full attention. I felt him moving beside me for half a second, making certain not to create any unnecessary noise like the footsteps that were approaching us.

Without looking at him, I flicked my left hand around, hoping that he would get the message that I wanted everyone else awake. I didn't want to be the only one responsible in this situation. Out of everyone, I wanted the Captain woken more than anyone else.

Slowly, I felt several pairs of ears suddenly prick up and for a moment it felt as though the footsteps had quietened, on account of the fact that I was now having to share the noise with the others.

McKay had slid down the front of the hole and was now somewhere behind me, along with Hamilton, Earnshaw and Chester.

At the lip of the hole were three apprehensive and confused faces; Captain Arnold, Sergeant Lawrence and me.

I tensed my whole body, as I readjusted my head so that my cheek rested comfortably on the butt of my rifle and slowly, I began to close one eye, so that I would be able to take a well-directed shot.

Lawrence must have sensed me wanting to fire out into the darkness and placed a hand gently on the barrel of my rifle. He leaned into me.

"Don't shoot. We'll give ourselves away. If we do that, then the whole game is up."

He spoke as few words as possible, while still able to get the same message across to me.

If you shoot, we are all dead.

"It's probably for the best, Andrew. Your aim has been off a little bit recently, hasn't it?"

Not now, Bob. Can't you see I'm busy?

I was growing tiresome of Bob's interjections in my life and it was inconvenient for me to be considering why his voice was appearing, when there was a German patrol on its way to meet me.

Nevertheless, I began to give some thought as to why he was there. I toyed with everything from sheer exhaustion, all the way to cowardice, but deep down I knew the real reason.

You lied to him. Not to his face, but you lied to him.

I had told myself, and promised Bob, that I would empty the contents of the hip flask on the floor the minute that I made it back. But I hadn't, and now Bob was haunting me to make sure that I followed through on my pledge.

I watched attentively, as Lawrence repeated to the Captain what he had said to me.

"Don't shoot. We'll give ourselves away. If we do that, then the whole game is up."

But there was a problem with following Sergeant Lawrence's command. If we did shoot, then we would end up dead. If we didn't shoot, then the boys sitting in the frontline trenches would be the ones who ended up dead.

I was incredibly grateful all of a sudden, that I was not the officer in charge of that decision.

12

The more that I tried to ignore the words that fluttered through my mind, the louder they grew, the more forceful they became. Slowly, they morphed from words that rang at the back of my mind, to a convicting order, an order that was compelling me to take action.

"Shoot! Come on, pull the trigger! Open fire!"

I had not yet got used to the fact that Bob was still living in my mind, and I frequently found myself looking about me, to see if any of the others had heard the spectral voice that tormented me at my most vulnerable of moments. The more I listened to him though, the more that I realised that there was something different to his voice, and not just in the sense that he was finally talking to me again. It was ever so slightly strained, with an almost whinge like quality to it, the kind of noise that a young child makes when they first fall out of a tree.

Somehow, somewhere, Bob's voice was indicating to me how in pain he truly was. He didn't want to be there, he didn't want to be watching over me for the rest of my life, he simply wanted me to take action on the one thing that I had promised him, shortly before he had died.

It took almost every ounce of my energy to attempt to ignore him, but I threw myself into trying to spot the approaching figures, which I was certain would eventually accompany the scraping noises that screamed throughout No Man's Land.

At one point, I was almost certain that I'd seen them, four hunched over and crouching figures, their heads so close to the ground that I was certain that they would eventually lose their balance, and crash headfirst into the mud. But, just as I was about to point them out to the Captain and Sergeant Lawrence, Bob began screaming in my head once again.

"The trigger!" He bellowed, "go on, squeeze it! That's your job!"

I blinked furiously, trying in earnest to separate the thoughts that I knew were merely hallucinations, from the ones that I knew were rational, the ones that I knew that I could trust.

Once Bob was out of the way I knew that I would be back up to my most effective. My finger, however, continued to twitch around the curved steel of the trigger and I thought about moving my hand away completely, in case the jerk of nerves suddenly caused me to eject a round.

Just as I thought that I had relinquished all pressure on the trigger, an almighty eruption sounded from the end of my rifle. I felt no rifle kick, no pummelling rifle butt into the shoulder, just a never-ending ringing in my ears that felt like it would go on forever.

I began to rebuke myself for being the one that once

again managed to get some members of his team killed. For a moment, I even considered calling myself even more effective than a German soldier, as I had managed to get that many of my own men killed.

But it was only as I began to look around at the fearful faces around me, that I realised it wasn't my rifle that had bucked and kicked, but that of Sergeant Lawrence, one of our Canadian companions. The very man who had told us not to fire.

He lay in between both the Captain and me, and for a moment we locked eyes with one another in a moment of total and utter disbelief. But before we could rebuke the Sergeant, or question his motives, he was already firing another round followed by another, which only confirmed that what he had done had been deliberate.

"Open fire! They're getting too close!"

There was a brief pause between the end of the sentence, before Captain Arnold and I did anything at all, but after that we began to pour rounds out of our rifles, that would surely keep up with any of the machine guns.

Once I had expended all my rounds, I slid down the hole and allowed Earnshaw to slide up in my place.

Just as I began to fumble around the darkness, trying to draw out the new selection of rounds to place in my rifle, a flare was suddenly sent up considerately, which allowed me to load my rounds in a much more efficient manner than had I been doing it in the darkness.

From where I lay, I could see that the flare now ignited the Germans, their shadows dancing around unpredictably, as the light dangled in the sky in a most unstable manner. I watched as a few of them dropped to the ground to cover themselves, while another few dropped to the ground completely involuntarily.

Rifle cracks and machine guns began to ignite on every side of me, and for a moment I felt like I was in the middle of the most terrific display of firepower that the Western Front had ever seen. Bullets began lethally fizzing through the air, cracking every now and then as it found something to bury itself into. I could not see any of the rounds themselves, but I could certainly hear them.

I was completely breathless for around thirty seconds, and I began to become lightheaded as I struggled to recall what it felt like to breathe normally. All the while, I could hear bullets zipping through the air and then ripping through human flesh, as another soul was surrendered to death himself.

Just as I began to feel more like myself again, the machine guns and rifle snaps from either side began to subside somewhat.

I was grateful for the enhanced silence, as every man who manned his station held his breath and waited for someone to be the first to make a move. As I slowly managed to calm myself down, I found my hands wiping tears away from my eyes. At first, I was surprised to see their presence on the palms of my hands, but quite quickly realised that I was becoming more and more volatile with every piece of action that I found myself involved in.

As I reopened my eyes following the final few swipes from my fingertips, I instantly locked eyes with Captain Arnold once again. But what I saw this time, did not fill me with confidence, nor was it a look of reassurance that I so often took from him.

This time, what I gleaned from the Captain's face drew nothing short of an almighty fury from the depths of my being. I couldn't quite understand it, but what I looked at made me burn with rage.

Captain Arnold was looking at me with forlorn little eyes, but more than that, he was shaking his head as he looked at me.

13

I tried my hardest to not let the disapproving look of Captain Arnold get to me, but it eventually did. I could not understand why he had stared at me in such a disapproving manner. I had done nothing wrong.

Had I?

I checked myself once more, replaying my actions from a few short moments ago, wondering what on earth I had done to have warranted such a glare as I had done. His eyes, that had invariably burned with a wildness that I had never seen from another man, had become diluted somewhat, and were threatening to send tears streaming down his grease-packed cheeks.

As I gave the whole thing some more consideration, I became totally incensed with myself that I had done something horrifically wrong. I had let the Captain down but, more than that, I couldn't for the life of me work out what. And in my mind, that was worse than knowing what it was.

I became even more furious with the Captain, who

simply carried on his duties as if nothing had happened at all, simply keeping watch at the lip of the shell hole like all we had done was merely switched watch. Everyone else, clearly content that the excitement was all over, went about their business in the hole, which was mainly trying to get back to sleep.

The serenity that was a picture on everyone else's faces began to make me seriously question that a firefight had even broken out at all. Maybe, I told myself, that was why Captain Arnold had shaken his head, maybe I had gone to fire my rifle with no apparent stimulus to my senses, and that I had almost given the game away.

But then the thought crossed my mind that Captain Arnold had not even been shaking his head at me. I had formulated much more extravagant and ludicrous hallucinations in my mind in recent weeks than that. Not least the voice that had now suddenly gone quiet the minute that everything else around me had exploded.

Bob was gone, I hoped for the last time.

Right now, you have far more pressing matters, Andrew.

I stared at the Captain, with the kind of animosity burning in the depths of my stomach that a young boy harbours over a far superior batsman than he. I glared at him for what felt like hours, absorbing all the contours and inflections in his face. His face was soft and smooth, none of which actually assisted in calming me down whatsoever.

I was completely incensed at the thought of how Captain Arnold had let me down, especially in plain view of everyone else.

It's that hip flask. He's had enough of it now.

I wouldn't have any of it, the focused and determined

half of my brain fighting with the paranoid side. I wasn't quite sure which side would win out.

I needed to prove to the Captain, and everyone else for that matter, that I wasn't simply here for the sake of it. I was there to add some worth to the team, a value to it that might mean that at least some of the others might make it back.

My face burned with such an intensity that I thought maybe a few minutes of quiet contemplation would be needed, before I uttered another word or carried out another task, that was how fearful I was of myself.

But I needed to sort this out now. I wanted the Captain to think that I was better than he was giving me credit for.

"We need to go out there. Make sure we got them all."

With those few hushed words, I felt like I had retaken control of all of my senses. I felt more like myself once again and I was sure that this time, I wouldn't even need a sip from the hip flask to get me through it.

The Captain shot me a quizzical, but equally furious look. The others merely turned their heads in an acknowledgement for me.

"We do not want any of them to make it back to their lines," I explained. "If any of them get back, as long as they have air in their lungs, they'll be able to tell someone where the rifle flashes came from. We'll have artillery on our heads in seconds. Lawrence here has already mentioned how both sides have this area zeroed in."

Captain Arnold's mouth began to twitch furiously, as if he wanted to suddenly begin erupting into some hate-fuelled rhetoric, but one that he knew would be far better off supressed. His eyes had changed again though, from the wild, naïve ones that I had loved, to a pair of eyes that seemed to burn with a rage that only a distant father could reserve for his delinquent son.

He scratched away at his chin as a means to calm himself down, shortly before locking himself away in the loneliest corner of his mind.

"It might already be too late," Earnshaw's usual cheerful and chipper tones dulled somewhat by the months of strain he had been under.

"What do you mean?"

"One or two might have made it back already. We'll be too late."

"We'd be better off to find out, don't you think? Rather than just sit here."

I didn't want to let my only good idea go to waste after what was at stake.

"We don't have to sit here," chimed in the burly Canadian voice of Sergeant Lawrence, he chanced a look over at Chester, who sat looking up at him like an obedient child. "We could head back now. Before it gets too ugly. No point sitting around here waiting to be killed."

"Wasn't that what we were doing anyway?"

It felt good to at least have McKay in my corner.

Lawrence continued, "It would more than likely be better to postpone. Fall back now while we still have some darkness and return at another time."

McKay didn't need a second to think that one through.

"Yeah, and what happens then? By the time we're back here, we could have another twenty young lads back there with their heads caved in."

Lawrence and Chester simultaneously pulled faces that said they knew we were right. We were going to have to carry on, there was no way around it.

I chanced a look across at Captain Arnold and was immediately filled with a sense of pride and smugness. His face had started to twitch even more than before, as if someone was passing an infrequent electrical current across his face.

He knew that I was right but, for some reason, he was not at all keen to show it. There was some unknown rationale as to why he thought that I had let him down.

Was it because I had let the Canadians pull the trigger first? Should I have alerted him as to what was going on before everyone else? Was it because I had disagreed with him about McKay?

I resolved that I would never find out and settled with the cracks that were slowly beginning to show between us.

"We need to go, Sir."

That got his back up even more. In fact, I was beginning to draw a strange sense of satisfaction and accomplishment from making him feel like this. Maybe he thought that I was jostling for the position of the leader of the group.

"Fine," he eventually croaked, "you better be quick. But we can't all go. You're taking McKay."

Oh great.

He must have been really mad at me, to be sending me out on a patrol with the only man in the team that he wanted dead by the end of the night. I was half expecting to be shot in the back as we slowly crawled from the hole.

But I knew that Captain Arnold wasn't the sort.

I nodded my head towards McKay, in a way that said, "Come on then, let's get this over with."

Obligingly, McKay followed, dragging his rifle beside him.

Carefully, our eyes open so wide that it felt like we would never be able to close them again, we pulled our way out of the relative safety of the hole, Chester propping the corrugated sheeting up an extra few inches.

I was instantly hit by the coolness of the night, which had been covered somewhat by the intertwining hot breath of a group of men in a very tight spot. I took a few deep, controlled breaths to acclimatise to my new environment, before continuing on as normal.

We moved silently, stopping every few yards to make sure that the other was keeping up and hadn't died a silent death of exposure.

In a way, I was perfectly happy that I was heading out there with McKay, as he was the only one that I felt that I could trust. He had a point to prove, to the Captain, to himself, but also the superior officers who would no doubt scrutinise his appeal in his court martial.

He needed to show them that he was a man made of tougher stuff, which, in my opinion, he had more than done since the little wobble out in No Man's Land.

This would be the moment that would make or break us, we had reached the fork in the road. If we went down the wrong path it could lead to total humiliation, embarrassment and almost certain death.

If we chose the correct one, then we would be on the road to full redemption, I was certain of it, but death was still a sombre certainty.

The weight of responsibility, not just for my own life,

but that of McKay's too, began to crush down heavily on my shoulders, as I gave it an increasing consideration.

Ignore it. It doesn't matter. Just leave it alone.

The quivering hands were back, and I was sure that even McKay could sense it, despite the fact that I was moving vast quantities of earth around as I pulled myself further across No Man's Land. The more I tried to steady my hands however, the fiercer the looming skull ache became.

If only I could just get a sip. Just one, I'm sure that would be enough.

The pain grew to an almost intolerable level and I began to consider the option of stopping there and then for the tiniest of sips.

I was surprised with myself, not because I was in the position of needing another sip of paraffin, but because of the fact that it had been so long since my last one. It had been at least four or five hours since my latest gulp. I was almost proud of myself for making it that far.

My thoughts were interrupted by a sudden and rather aggressive nudge in the ribs. I jumped, flicking my head over to McKay to see what it was that had caught his attention.

He pointed straight ahead of us and I could almost hear his silent, Scot voice whisper in my imagination.

"There, over there. See?"

I followed his finger, where I could just about make out a faint outline, that looked more like a mound of earth than anything that we were looking for, but at long last, I began to make out the brief features of a man.

There was definitely a head and shoulders lying there in the dirt, but after that, I could not make out much else.

It was time to approach them even more cautiously than we had been doing. We couldn't afford to make a single sound.

I poked back into McKay's ribs, giving him a taste of his own medicine. He stared at me, his huge, infant-like eyes staring back at me, that screamed of nothing more than sheer obedience.

Using nothing but fast, accusing finger tips, I pointed out to him where he should and where I should go.

I did not like to do it, as it felt like I was cutting off my own arm, but also severing myself from any real chance of survival.

But I knew, as did McKay, that we simply had to do it.

So, reluctantly, we began to crawl in opposite directions.

14

As I moved stealthily about No Man's Land, occasionally coming across a body that looked like it had been there far longer than a few minutes, I began to appreciate the slowly changing colours of the horizon far in the distance. The midnight black that had gripped this part of the world for a good six or seven hours, was slowly becoming tainted in the distance, as if an ink pot had been spilled some way off and we were only now seeing the effects of it.

I stopped for a moment and for a while simply enjoyed my own company in the serenity of No Man's Land. I found it odd, as I lay there, the cold seeping through onto my chest, that man could try so hard to destroy Mother Nature and all her beauty and yet, all of our efforts were eclipsed by the stunning simplicity of the sun slowly appearing over the horizon.

As I breathed in a few long and contented breaths, for the first time in a long time, I felt something that could quite easily have been mistaken for happiness, joy almost. It comforted me somewhat that no matter how much these soldiers wanted to kill and maim one another, no matter how many trees they wanted to see flattened to the ground, the sunrise, in all its stubbornness, would do its utmost every morning to remind its admirers that there was still a beauty to the world, one that mankind could never get hold of and therefore never destroy.

I sighed what felt like a sigh of relief and pleasure at the thought, which involuntarily morphed into a low, verging on desperate, growl.

Careful now. This is not the right time to lose focus.

But, at that moment, my head began to pound with such a ferociousness that I thought my skull would split open and pour itself all over the field that was trying its best to freeze me to death.

Go on. You're alone now, no one can see.

I did as I was told.

GRHMN.

Oh, that tastes good.

I had another, followed by another.

That should be enough for now. The headache's already subsiding.

In my appreciation for the gradual changing colours of the sky and my brief stop off for a quick drink, I had lost all sense of where I was and how long I had been there.

Instantly, I began to flap.

What if McKay was already heading back to the hide? What if he had decided that I had been lost and was not worthy of being found? More importantly, what if he had suspected a conspiracy between both the

Captain and me, and he was now lining up the sights of his rifle?

I looked around me, to see if I could see him from somewhere, but the darkness still held fast, to such a degree, that it was almost impossible to conceive that someone would be able to take a well-aimed rifle shot.

I was safe, for now.

I moved around erratically, trying to find the one person that resembled something of a friend in this bizarre war.

But almost straight away, I stopped.

The low growl, the threatening one that had spontaneously whistled from my lips, had returned. Somewhere ahead of me and slightly over to my right.

From where I was, I could see nothing. I was going to have to go and investigate it for myself.

Maybe then, the Captain wouldn't appear so disappointed in me, if he was to know what I had done for him.

The low growling gradually morphed into more of a grunt, which itself turned into something far more sinister than a meaningless brush of air over a man's vocal chords.

Someone was fighting.

I tried to remain as calm as possible, all the while becoming increasingly nervy as to who it was that was in a tussle. One of the combatants had to be McKay, it simply had to be him. He was in some sort of trouble.

My heart now thumping out of my chest, to the point where I thought the faraway artillery had suddenly woken up, I dragged myself through the mud, soaking my skin and muddying every inch of my face. I didn't care about how much dirt I ate, or what was lurking within it. My best friend needed me.

I slowed somewhat as the grunts became even more audible, until the point where I barely seemed to move at all. I wanted to make sure that I had got this right and that I would still be able to withdraw silently if I hadn't.

I peered in a depression in the ground and could instantly make out a lone figure as he stumbled around on all fours. He made his way over to another figure, who was clearly in a worse state than the predator above him.

Just as the first figure tried to bring something down hard on the other's head, the second man rolled over to one side, with a perfect timing, that sent the bayonet plunging into the mud.

The second man, the one that had rolled, was none other than Christopher McKay. It was the first time that I had ever seen him begin to lose a fight.

Without any consideration for where I was, I leapt to my feet, and threw myself into the hole and towards the bayonet-wielding German.

The butt of my rifle, the only weapon I really had to hand, connected wonderfully with the back of his neck, which sent him jolting forward as if he had been stunned in some way.

He wrangled and wrestled below me, as I tried to bring the rifle down on him again, but I was forced to throw myself over to one side. He had managed to wangle his right arm free and was now wildly launching his bayonet behind his back, in a most unnatural fashion, trying to catch me in any way that he possibly could.

He rolled over and instantly began to make his way

over to me, the figure with nothing to protect him other than a rifle that he knew I could not use.

Come on, McKay. Do something.

The German tumbled towards me and I could do nothing but watch his ever-growing silhouette as it loomed larger over me, like something out of a nightmare.

Come on, Fritz. I came over to save you, what are you doing?

The bayonet plunged down on me, and I barely thought as I flicked my rifle over from right to left to deflect the blow. By sheer good fortune, as it was certainly not skill, the bayonet was suddenly flung from the German's hand, the moment of realisation recorded perfectly within the whites of his eyes.

I've got you now. You're mine.

I kicked out at him, catching perfectly where no man ever wants to be caught, which sent him crashing to the ground in an instant. To his credit, he remained the consummate professional, not even uttering a harsh word in my direction, nor even a shriek. He didn't want to draw any attention to any of this any more than we did.

My rifle came down hard on the back of his head once more, which resounded with the most sickening crack that I had ever heard before in my life, and I was surprised to see that he was still conscious after it.

He was slower though, groggy, which allowed me a few seconds of fumbling around, to allow me to find the very bayonet that he had been threatening me with just moments before.

I was thankful that the man kept his head down in the dirt as I found the bayonet, as I plunged it into his skin, right about where I thought his throat was, applying the full weight of my body behind it to make sure that he sustained the worst wound possible. I still tried to convince myself that it was done out of compassion more than anything.

I pressed down so hard, and gave it a firm little twist, that I managed to pin the bloke to the ground.

He was gone. I was still alive.

Now, where was McKay? Why hadn't he bothered to help me?

I wasted no time in trying to compose myself or get my breath back, I wanted an answer immediately.

There was another body in the hole with us, another German, who looked like he had been dead some time before I had got there. It was next to the rotting corpse of the young German that McKay sat, wincing tightly as he tried to address his own situation.

He made no attempt to thank me for saving his life, or even simply coming to find him, but I wasn't even sure he knew who I was at that moment in time.

Even in the darkness, and under all the layers of grease and dirt that was packed to his skin, I could tell that he was losing what was left of the very pale pigment in his face. Underneath all of his layers, he was as white as a sheet.

Embedded in the top of his arm, alarmingly close to where his chest was, was a long, ghoulish dagger that had been pushed in firmly through McKay's skin. It was producing a lot of blood and McKay was already trying his hardest to remove it from its housing place.

I was suddenly awash with guilt as I stared down at his helpless body.

"You've done this," he said to me, "You could have helped me sooner."

The words did not actually fall from McKay's mouth, nor did I even imagine them doing so, but instead his harsh Scottish sounds were replaced by something far softer, but far more harrowing.

Bob Sargent.

As ever, I looked around me, and then down at my hands, that were now covered in a thin layer of the German's blood, on top of hour old dirt and muck. That was exactly how I liked them, as it reminded me that I was still alive.

But the one thing that I did notice about my hands, which I did not care for in the slightest, was the fact that they were not quivering. They were as steady as a surgeon's.

The drink. The hip flask. You took too long.

This time, there was no need for Bob Sargent to rebuke me, as I was doing a pretty good job of it myself as I stared at my filthy palms.

If only you hadn't had a sip. If only you had got here quicker, then maybe McKay wouldn't be looking like this right now.

I didn't know what to do. So, I did the only thing that I was used to doing.

GRHMN.

Only then, did I feel like I had the courage to stand up to what I had done.

"You okay, McKay? Can you hear me?"

15

Fortunately, McKay was only wounded in the arm and, although he had lost a large amount of blood, he was still capable of being able to drag himself back towards the Canadian's lair.

He seemed quite calm, as if everything that occupied his mind was on his arm and making sure that he didn't leave a trail of blood back to our hidey hole. Which was the least of our problems at that moment in time, as I wasn't entirely sure where the hole was and considered for a moment making a brisk dash back to our frontline. But I knew I wouldn't even last a second in the event.

I began to flap and panic, keeping my stomach pressed down as low into the ground as it would possibly go, but keeping my head up as high as I dared. I scoured everything around me.

There was nothing. Nothing that I recognised and nothing that I could use as any sort of reference. For all I knew, we had been going around in circles for the last fifteen minutes.

I searched desperately for the piece of corrugated iron to suddenly lift and reveal itself to me, to the point where my eyes wanted to stream with water as they burned as if a branding iron had been pressed into my pupils.

I was becoming increasingly concerned too, for the amount of light that was beginning to tickle the horizon in the distance. The midnight blue of the night was slowly being taken over by a lighter shade of its former self, as the sun began to work its way up and above the horizon.

It wouldn't be all that long before the horizon burned an intense orange, and everything around me would be completely visible to a naked eye. It would also be around about now, when the German sentries were called up to their posts, readying themselves for the morning stand-to.

In under an hour, there could quite easily be over a hundred rifles all trained on me and McKay, which carried odds of survival at less than zero.

We needed to find the Canadian's hideout, and fast.

I turned, to quickly check on McKay's progress, and to make sure that he hadn't passed out in the thirty seconds or so since I had last checked on him.

I peered over my left shoulder, just as a hand gripped firmly around my right ankle, with such an aggression that I thought I would lose my foot. I daren't turn around, but eventually knew that I had to.

A hand had appeared from out of the ground, a dry and cracked hand, with nails so long that a thick layer of dirt and grime had settled underneath them. It had been a long time since they had seen a bar of soap.

Reluctantly, I followed the hand, looking up the dirtied and muddied arm, to see who, or what, it was connected to.

I panned round, following up the figure's chest and began to catch sight of the stubble that had come to rest on the man's chin.

His mouth was creased and gave off the impression that it had almost been worn down over the years, as if his skin was incredibly thin. The valleys and wrinkles that were etched over his skin were not permanent, but had increased in their depth on account of the huge grin that was stretched across the lower quadrant of his face.

"Gotcha."

"You're a stupid fool, Lawrence. I could have killed you."

"I would have killed you first."

He gripped my hand and dragged me through the slit in the hide, which opened up into the most welcome sight I could have hoped for. The rest of the team were all still there. McKay, grunting and squawking was dragged in behind me by Chester.

"What happened to you?" chirped one of the Canadians at the sight of McKay, I couldn't quite tell which one, as I was still so bewildered by their accents that their voices morphed into one.

"I got a knife in my arm. Help me, would you?"

The Captain shot me an accusing and nervous look. I could imagine exactly what was going through his mind.

Close. But not quite good enough.

It was almost as if he was proud of me for letting McKay get himself wounded, but also equally disappointed that I had managed to help bring him back. In the next second though, the guilt was awash over his face and for the first time he began to come to a realisation of what he had said to me and how it all must have looked.

For the time being, the shaking of his head and his disapproval of me, had suddenly vanished. He was my Captain once again, the vulnerable one who liked to be reminded of his own mortality from time to time.

"You okay, Sir?" I asked him, trying to force him out from the trance that he found himself in.

His head jolted, as he wiped away the visions and meanderings that were beginning to slow him right down.

"We don't have time for this," he suddenly blurted. "The sun's on its way up."

"Nearly showtime," croaked Sergeant Lawrence, who left McKay to be tended by Hamilton and plonked himself down on the other side of the hole.

"Exactly. We can't take him anywhere, he's in a bad way." He looked over at McKay, whose blood flow had been stemmed somewhat, but the effect of the loss of his vital bodily fluid was beginning to take hold on him. His face had paled to such a degree that I was certain that the dirt packed onto his skin would slowly be absorbed too, as if everything around him would be sucked in to replace what he had lost.

I needed a drink, not because of the headache or the quivering hands, but simply because I wanted one. More than that, I felt like I deserved one. I didn't even care what anyone thought of me anymore, once I had made my mind up to withdraw it, I was going to be taking a nice long sip and allow the liquid to burn at every single one of my insides, on its way to the stomach.

I reached up, to run my hand around the outside of the hip flask before withdrawing it.

GRHMN.

But I wasn't able to turn the flask over in my palm and read the letters, as something had changed, which stopped me dead in my tracks.

The flask was gone.

Immediately, I began to flap, throwing the pocket open and rummaging around inside aggressively as I ran my hand inside the empty lining. The fabric felt rough on my delicate and worn hands, but they never once hit the polished steel of the hip flask.

It was definitely gone.

I looked around me, to see if any of the others were sitting there smirking at me, having pinched it from me while I was asleep, but there were no such faces, just faces of confusion and bewilderment.

The hip flask was gone. The one that had been with me ever since Sergeant Needs had handed it to me many months before.

I should have expected this day to come, what with the job that I was being asked to do, but I had never given it a great deal of consideration.

I began trying to retrace my movements, in the hope that I might have subconsciously remembered something that would tell me it was only a few feet away, or that it was tightly tucked up under my pillow back in our billet.

But there was nothing. I could remember nothing. Without it, it seemed, my brain could not function correctly at all.

Suddenly, I locked eyes with Captain Arnold, who

immediately sensed my distress and tried to give me a comforting look in return. It did not work.

My heart, now thumping out of my chest, felt like it would burst at any moment, in response to the sudden separation, and my breathing became more erratic and shallower as I began to succumb to the panic.

It wasn't so much the liquid inside that was causing me all the distress, as I knew that I would be able to get bottles of the stuff the minute that we returned, but it was the small container that I had housed it in, the one that had seen me through for months, that was now making me hyperventilate.

"What's wrong with him?" asked a voice, from somewhere, as my eyesight began to haze.

The hip flask had become a talisman, a charm, one that had kept me alive all this time. I was convinced that whoever held it in their possession would be kept alive by some guardian angel, as it had done with Sergeant Needs for many years, until he had passed it onto me. I was convinced of its validity as I knew full well that it was not down to any ability on my part that I had managed to survive this war so far. Without it, I was certain that I would be dead by the time the sun had come up.

"It's his hip flask," Captain Arnold muttered in reply to the voice.

"So what?" It had to be one of the Canadians, everyone else knew how important it was to me. "He can have a drink later."

"It's not like that," argued the Captain, defiantly. "He needs it. We need it. It brings us good fortune."

"There is no fortune in war. We're here, that's proof that it doesn't exist in my book."

"We're not reading your book, Sergeant," the Captain suddenly exploded, so loud that the corrugated iron began to shiver. As he screamed, everyone fell silent, hastily pulling fingers over triggers in preparation for something to happen.

Nothing did. Even I stopped breathing for a moment. It was what was needed.

I began to calm myself down.

It's just an object. How could it possibly be the thing keeping you alive? No German has missed because of that flask. No shrapnel has flown passed me because of it.

We remained in a silence for a good while longer, each of us thinking through what was going to happen now our talisman was gone.

The Captain, in particular, looked even more anxious than before. I wondered if he had had a change of heart and had been hoping that I might lend it to McKay until we made it back, to keep him safe.

"We need to get going with this plan," Lawrence suddenly announced, smashing the silence into a thousand pieces.

Maybe it would be good for all of us to remember why we were really there. We had a job to do and one that only had a small window. We couldn't all sit there and dwell on a missing hip flask.

"Right...Yes," stumbled the Captain, as he tried to recoup his senses and intuition that had got him to where he was.

"So, basic plan is for you chaps to draw the sniper out so that we can spot and take him out. Then, hopefully, you can get close enough to retrieve the rifle and anything else that our officers wanted."

"That means you'll need to be quick after we take him. He'll likely have his own observer who will try to get the rifle back," Chester's thoughtful and precise tones graced my ears. It was nice to know that there was someone there who had taken great thought and consideration to everything. Somehow, it made me feel ever so slightly more positive about the whole thing. Even though I was convinced that I would be dead before the sun found its full strength.

"Two minutes then, chaps. We'll move then. Make ready."

As one, we began checking our pouches were full and that rifles were ready for the off. Silently, I thought I could see Hamilton muttering some kind of a prayer and in the corner of the shell hole, squashed into an impossibly small space between the two Canadians, was Bob Sargent.

He was there staring at me, with a slight smile just bending at the corners of his mouth, in the same way that the sun was slowly making its way up from under the horizon. Still keeping his gaze fixed on mine, he lifted up his left hand and gently kissed his ring finger.

It was something that he hadn't done in a while, but I took more comfort and warmth from that one small hallucination of my mind, than I had ever done from a sip of the hip flask.

For the first time since becoming a soldier, I felt ready. I felt prepared to die in the next few hours.

"I should come," groaned McKay, as he fumbled around and tried to take possession of his rifle once again.

I looked across at Captain Arnold, who was already

staring at me expectantly. If he was to carry out his desires, he would allow McKay to come with us, the nature of his injury rendering him so useless that maybe he would get himself killed by the German sniper.

He barely even looked at McKay as he spoke, instead choosing to keep his eyes fixed on me as he mumbled his orders.

"No, Christopher. You're to stay here, with these two. We'll risk too much if you were to come with us. You need to stay as still as possible for the time being."

McKay didn't even try to put up any kind of resistance, instead opting to simply sink back into the dirt and close his eyes, dejected. It seemed like that was exactly what he had wanted to have heard.

I was worried about him.

"Everyone ready?" I asked, my voice so dishevelled and cracked that I thought someone else had possessed my vocal chords.

There were no mutters of agreement, no nods of the head in confirmation, just a determined stare from every man that I looked at.

"Okay then, let's get a move on."

As I made my way out of the shell hole, Chester kindly lifting the lid for us to slide out like a colony of snakes, I turned back to breathe in Lawrence's ear.

"Look after him and, whatever you do, don't miss."

He scoffed at me and whispered back, a hint of excitement in the back of his throat.

"We're Canadians, mate. Not Brits. We don't miss."

And, with that, the iron sheeting was gently lowered back to the ground, and we were alone in No Man's Land.

Just how we all liked it.

16

The sun slowly began to grow in strength, its petals unfurling gradually like a flower in bloom. It was as I stared at it, in its more infant-like, weakened state, that I began to realise how much I had always taken it for granted.

It was always there, to warm me, to comfort me and, even when I could not see it, I could feel its effects every time that I found myself outside of a building.

I recalled that, as a child, I would play a foolish game with my sister, the blonde-haired girl that I had frequently forgotten. We would end up in some field somewhere, normally hiding up a tree or buried in some sort of undergrowth.

We would spend hours staring at the sun, trying to see who could hold its gaze the longest before being forced to turn away, eyes streaming with more tears than a November rainfall.

I looked up at it now, just appearing to the east and hundreds of miles behind the German frontline. It pained my eyes to look at it, but I did not falter, but instead let the tears rush to my eyes before falling to the ground.

Everything around me seemed to burn an orange for minutes afterwards, a complete contrast to the blank canvas of charcoal that had been my obsession for the hours before.

Only now, with the ever-increasing strength of the sun, was I able to look around me and get my first few glances at this section of the line. It was then that I realised how vastly different the terrain was to *Le Plantin* and how everything was different here.

The ground, No Man's Land in particular, was completely flat, like a bowling green that had been scorched black. But, a few miles behind the German frontline, which was a similar mess of contorted concrete and barbed wire, was a large hill, that rose high into the air and obstructed the sun in large chunks.

It was ideal, I supposed, to place at least one battery of artillery, as it allowed for an incredible field of fire right the way across the British frontline and large chunks of No Man's Land. It reminded me of a cliff that I had once seen as a child, that seemed to grow and grow to the point where it had simply given up, and I wondered if the sheer drop on the other side resembled anything like the coastline of Britain that I had seen when I was a young boy.

I wondered, not for very long, but long enough to distract myself from the war around me, whether I would be able to see a small German battery commander, standing next to his guns, if I was to use a naval-like tele-scope for just a few minutes.

I even toyed with the idea that there was already a man up there, looking down at my confused little face, as I stared almost directly at him. I quickly changed my face to one that pleaded with him not to fire upon us just yet.

If he was even there.

It was as I looked around me that I realised how perfect the conditions were for everything that could go against us. Mother Nature seemed to be on the Germans' side, as did the positioning of their lines and guns.

The guns that were atop the hill would be able to fire with no threat from our own guns, with such a perfect vision all around that on a clear day it wouldn't have surprised me if they could see us all the way back in Albert.

As the sun came up too, it would be the German sniper's paradise.

The sun rose gently from behind the German lines, which made it incredibly difficult for any British soldier to see where it was exactly the German rounds were coming from, never mind the possibility of some return fire. The sniper would remain completely unchallenged.

The positioning of the sun, combined with the time of day, would mean that the sharpshooter would have a plethora of targets to choose from this morning, I was certain of it.

The morning stand-to had likely already been called and, if the German sharpshooters really did have specially built and new sights to look down, then I was sure they would be able to see more tiny heads bobbing above the parapet than they would normally do.

It was perfect conditions for them.

For a moment, I felt incredibly jealous of them, the

way that they would be able to pick off targets with almost no chance of being fired upon in return. They were safe.

That was however, until I realised that come evening, the shoe would well and truly be on the other foot and, with any luck, it would be Lawrence and Chester who were doing the unchallenged sharpshooting in this sector of the frontline.

It wouldn't be too long before the German sniper, with the conditions playing so far in his favour, reared his ugly head and began to give some of our boys a headache. It was all just a waiting game.

If all else failed with the operation, then at least we would hopefully be able to draw the sharpshooter's fire away from our boys just long enough so that they could get a bit of a break. The thought continued to grow in validity in my own mind, as I began to convince myself that my time was nearly up.

Over the last few weeks I had seen my best friend, possibly my only friend that I had ever really known, being killed right before my eyes, with a large portion of the blame resting on my shoulders. I had seen the men around me slowly turn on each other and now, one of my only other friends had taken a hit to his arm and was in a bad way and faced a firing squad even if he was to pull through.

It seemed like everyone around me was slowly being killed or wounded, and that it was only me that had avoided the real realities of war. But now, my hip flask was gone.

I thought back to Sergeant Needs, who had told me to hold onto the flask until after the advance. But, halfway through, I had found him with a round in the side of his head and his eyes glazed over as if the round itself had severed all the connections in his eye socket.

I tried to think back to the night that he had given it to me and wondered if there was anything in his face that could have told me how he was feeling. Was there any sense of regret as he passed it to me? Had he done it deliberately because he knew it would keep me safe? Or was it all in my mind? Maybe there was no keeping powers in the hip flask whatsoever.

Maybe I had just been fortunate up until this point.

Either way, I still felt like I would die before lunchtime.

As Captain Arnold withdrew the leather-bound notebook that had been a gift on Earnshaw's return from the hospital, my attention began to turn to McKay. I wondered how he was doing, and I hoped desperately that the Canadians were doing their absolute best for him. But I was aware that, in reality, they had a job to do, a far more important one than simply keeping McKay alive, and so I resorted to half-prayer, half-plea to anyone that had any influence, that McKay would somehow still be alive when we tried to regroup with the Canadians.

If you live that long.

I pictured him asleep for a while, his small, childlike face, still untouched by the blemishes of adulthood, moving around gently as he softly snored. It was a picture that I needn't have to engage my imagination for too much, as it was burned into my memory, after many sleepless nights. His was the only face that I really cared to look at and appreciate.

I was grateful for him, I would tell myself each time,

and the way in which he conducted himself. He was a hard fighter, a brilliant one, but one who had a host of problems the minute that he stepped back into the safety of a British trench.

He was constantly nervous, and always looking for a way out, he was never able to think things through all that much and had come close to all-out desertion.

But all of this, his flaws and shortcomings, only taught me how to behave myself. Away from the action, McKay had problems, as did I. I was reckless and uncaring, selfish and had more than a slight dependency on alcohol.

But outside of the wire, McKay was a brilliant fighter, pushing all the hindrances away from him to the point where he was prepared to have a knife embedded in him, for the good of the operation.

It was on that basis that I had taught myself to think. I had taught myself to be a soldier based on McKay's example.

Away from the frontline, behave how you like, just as long as when it matters, you are able to step up.

Captain Arnold coughed gently, which startled me to the point where I thought I might wet myself. He shuffled over to me, nervously, sliding down the hole that we were in so that his mouth aligned with my ear.

"About McKay. I changed my mind. I was tired, exhausted. I did not really know what I was saying. I was awfully flustered."

I lifted my hand up towards his face to try and stop him.

"You don't need to explain, Terence. We are all in the

same boat. We're knackered, no one makes rational decisions when we're like that."

He tried to speak again, so I simply reiterated the hand, but this time, he swatted it away, as if it were an irritating summer fly.

"No, you don't understand. I was tired, yes. But it doesn't excuse what I said."

"Sir, I don't care what you said to me, really I—"

"What I said to you? Oh no, I'm not talking about that. I'm on about what I said to the blokes in charge of McKay's court martial."

I gave him a look which told him that I had had a change of heart, and now I wanted him to spill the beans immediately.

"I went to see them. To persuade them to drop the case, to prove to them that I needed him. I was hoping that they would erase the charges, but they didn't. I wanted them to give McKay the option to find an honourable way out. If he goes to court martial, it will be quick for McKay, but for his parents they'd lose everything.

"Honestly, they would. My family employ people like his family. It is based entirely on conduct and honour. His father would lose his job as gamekeeper. His mother would no longer be one of the housemaids."

I looked at him perplexed. I hadn't even known that his mother was still alive, let alone what she did for a living.

"What did you say to them, Sir? You need to tell me."

He closed his notebook rather too heavily, the pages giving a muted thud as he clasped his hands together, checking around him to make sure that Hamilton and

Earnshaw were keeping watch and were not listening in.

"I may have promised them something. Something which I am wholeheartedly regretting now, may I add."

"Sir?" I asked warily. I tried to prepare myself for what was coming, but equally I did not want to hear the words come from his mouth. As he began to utter them, I began to fill in his words from the first breath that carried the syllables along my ear.

"I promised them that if they let him come with us, that he would die at some point tonight. In combat. With honour to his name. I even got them to consider him for a posthumous medal of some sort."

I stared at him in horror and disbelief.

As I looked at him, his face began to morph, into something that I no longer recognised. The man before me had changed incredibly. It was almost as if the man that I had known before, the one who was so fiercely loyal to his men, to the point where he would hide their crimes, was wiped from the face of the earth. And now, all that sat in front of me was the epitome of evil, a conspiring devil.

He showed no external signs of being distressed or upset at this information, but the exhaustion littered across his face was able to tell me that on the inside it was burning him up ferociously. I almost began to feel sorry for him.

But I had no words that I could comfort him with.

"It also meant that you lot would be off the hook. For not mentioning anything, I mean."

"You lot?"

He scoffed, before reopening his notebook.

"It's a letter. To my parents," he said, showing me page after page of his scrawl. "It's explaining everything to them and why I did it. And to apologise to them."

"But why?"

"If McKay was killed tonight, then it was me who was the one that would stand in the dock. Instead of him. All part of the deal that was struck."

I was completely dumbfounded. Despite the worn-down appearance of his face and demeanour, it seemed like the fiercely loyal Captain was still there, hidden under all the layers of tiredness and stress.

As Hamilton took his turn up on watch, we sat in peacefulness for a while. In that moment, I knew exactly what the Captain was thinking, and he knew what was going through my own mind.

For now, at least, a truce existed between us. We were, once again, an officer and his sergeant, in perfect tune with one another.

17

I continued to observe Captain Arnold, simply making a mental note over everything that he did, from a slight sniffle at around five in the morning, to a readjustment of how he was lying just ten minutes later.

I wondered why he had started to divulge the information about McKay with me, and what kind of thoughts had raced through his mind to lead him up to it. I was certain that what had happened with the hip flask had something to do with it, as the stress lines on his face had seemed to have deepened greatly in the few hours or so that I had discovered that I had lost it.

The Captain, as rational and level-headed as he appeared was, in actual fact, far more superstitious over small, insignificant objects like that than I was. Maybe he wanted to die as a man that had told the truth in his final few hours.

In some ways, I thought that what he had said to me was grossly unfair as now, I not only had to live with the knowledge that Captain Arnold had struck up a bargain behind everyone's back, but I would now have to look McKay in the eye and know that he came within an inch of being betrayed by his own officer.

If either of us make it back.

Although McKay was not with us, and therefore significantly safer than he would be, there was still a worryingly high chance that he would be dead by the time we made it back to the Canadians, either as a result of his wounds, or by the hands of the Canadians themselves, who I still could not trust entirely.

As I stared the Captain down however, I began to feel desperately sorry for him, and I began to search myself as to why that was. At first, it was because of his situation and how he had been ripped away from the girl that he had wanted to marry, but was now dwelling on it daily, gradually coming to terms of her life continuing without him being by her side. I wondered if she was giving as much thought to him as he was to her, or whether she had already moved on with her life with some other rich, well-connected aristocrat.

But, as I continued to stare at his exhausted and timid features, I began to question what else I would have done, had I been in his position. I tried to place myself in his shoes, which amused me for a while, as his feet must have been twice the size of my own.

I wondered if I would have tried to plead for McKay's life and whether or not I would have even come up with the same idea as he had done, to think past McKay for a moment and consider his family. Even if McKay was found innocent, the word would soon reach his family and hometown and the entire family name would become ostracised.

As I thought about it, I came to the realisation that McKay must avoid a court martial at all costs, but for the life of me I could see no way around it, as I did not for a second give any consideration to having him killed deliberately.

Each and every avenue I came down though was inconclusive, I didn't know what to do at all. There was one thing that the Captain had done that I would have changed immediately, however. I would have made sure that I told my sergeant immediately of my intentions and what the plan was, there would simply be no secrets between us.

In that regard, I still felt ever so slightly betrayed by Captain Arnold. But, then again, he was an officer and he was given the authority by the King himself to keep such things hidden from men like me.

As I continued to try and fit my feet into the loose-fitting boots of the Captain, I began to rack my brains to see if I could think of anything that might mean McKay, and everyone else, got out of the predicament that we were in.

Suddenly, my mind reminded me of the conversation that I had had with Hamilton, in the middle of the night without anyone seeing or hearing it. I thought now might have been a good time to gently remind him of my proposal, before thinking better of it.

He needed to have his mind completely focused on what was going on around him. He was not quite like the rest of us yet, who cared so little for our own lives that we allowed ourselves to be distracted by what we would do should we survive.

There was a slight possibility that Hamilton had

already written the letter, and a small piece of paper, with a grovelling apology and desperate plea scrawled across it, was sitting on the desk of his father's office in the Admiralty.

I tried not to get too excited by the prospect, as the letter may even have made things worse by now and as soon as we made it back, we would all be carted off to a prison cell somewhere, to be shot without trial.

Nevertheless, I resolved with myself to apply even more pressure onto Hamilton when we made it back, to make sure that he felt compelled to write the letter. I had no grievances in coming across as a vicious and aggressive man, if it meant that one member of the team would still be with us this time next week.

You'll only be able to do that if you make it back.

I rebuked myself once more for becoming distracted in the nature that I had done and instead tried to focus wholeheartedly on what it was that I was meant to be doing. But my heart had other ideas altogether.

I simply had to do everything that I could for McKay, starting by getting him back to our frontline and into some hospital somewhere. At least that would buy him a little more time, while he recuperated in hospital somewhere, as that meant that the court martial simply couldn't go ahead.

I began to run through all sorts of possibilities in my head, a daring escape from prison perhaps, or bare-faced lying in front of a military court, each idea exciting me even more than the last. The one thought that recurred each and every time in the process, however, was the fact that I couldn't lose another friend.

Especially losing one when I felt like I could have done more to keep him alive.

I had already surrendered my friendship with Bob, and I would simply not do the same with McKay, I needed him by my side for as long as possible. I could not live with myself if McKay was lost just as Bob had been.

I began to wish with every ounce of my energy that Bob would somehow be reinstated, to help me fight McKay's corner, even though we were all silently convinced that it had been Bob who had started this whole process off.

Who else would it have been?

Not McKay, as he would have known the consequences of handing himself in. Not Earnshaw as he had no reason to. Sergeant Hughes? Maybe. He was the honest sort, but he would have known the consequences.

Everything seemed to point to Bob.

But still I felt an enduring sense of loyalty to him, despite the fact he might have condemned me to a lengthy prison spell.

All these things I continued to consider in a great detail, and in far greater depth than I ever had done before, to the point where I thought that hours simply must have passed in the time that I had taken to mull them over.

In reality however, I was not entirely sure how long I had been asleep for, I was simply aware of the fact that at some point, in the not so distant past, I had been.

Sometimes, very rarely, when I would sleep, I had the knack of waking up just before an event; an alarm clock ring, or a door being shut extraordinarily loudly. If I was aware of how to do it, then I would do it far more frequently, but in my experience, there was nothing more to it other than simply waking up.

There must be some sort of human nature to sense a change in the air pressure just before the vibrations of the noise reverberate down your ear canal, but for the life of me I could not understand why. Maybe it was for our ancestors who had to run for their lives, shortly after a lion's bellow, or possibly for the sleeping scoundrel on the streets at the sound of a Peeler's whistle.

I did not know. All I knew is that I woke up just a nanosecond before the gunshot cracked out over No Man's Land.

It was the first time that I had been conscious of the fact that I was asleep. There was no real time in between me waking up and the shot ringing out, it simply happened the minute I regained consciousness.

The gunshot itself seemed to spit across No Man's Land, as if it was the vilest thing that it had ever set its eyes upon. I immediately thought of Edmund Tapper, the large imposing bully in the schoolyard, who had forcefully spat over me after I had lost our latest boxing bout.

It was the vilest thing that anyone, or anything, could do in my opinion, which was why I instantly found myself hating that gunman, the one who had spat towards the British frontline.

The sound echoed dully across the landscape, as if the desolation and flatness, that came with No Man's Land, somehow assisted in encouraging the noise to carry on as far away as possible.

I wondered how many other men had heard it and how many had flinched or ducked the second that they had heard the crack. I began to think too of the man that the round may have struck, who would now be lying at the bottom of a slightly damp trench, clutching at his wound if he was lucky, or silently accepting of it, if he was not.

I felt the air around me change as the round itself began to carve its way through the early morning mist, towards one of the bobbing heads as they perched on the fire step and peered out with periscopes.

I prayed desperately that maybe this one had missed and that now we could get on with our job, that none of the other spitting rounds would be towards our boys in the frontline.

I wondered if they knew we were out here. I hoped that they were willing us to success.

As soon as the echoing had ceased, and everyone in our little hidey hole had realised that they were still alive, we all sat upright, our muscles tensed and ready for action. I felt the blood begin to surge around my body, much faster than before, to the point where I could feel my legs and arms burn, despite the fact that I had barely used them in hours.

My body was raring to go.

I looked around me.

Captain Arnold was ready.

Hamilton was ready.

Earnshaw was ready.

This was it, this was everything that we had been waiting for. As a team, we had a lot to prove. Above everything, we had to prove our worth, that way, we might be able to get McKay off the hook.

I imagined the sobering thud of a brass round ripping through human flesh, just as the noises of men rushing around and calling out for a stretcher bearer could just about be heard, muffled, but still audible, from the British frontline.

Someone had copped the round and suddenly, I could not rid myself of the man who had been struck in the neck less than a week ago.

His skin had been pulled apart like a pair of curtains in the theatre, ready to display the cast of internal tubes and a mess of blood. It was an image that I would not be forgetting in a hurry.

As we made our weapons ready and huddled together like a pack of scared children, I could not get the other man's screams out of my mind, the one that had become stuck in my mind ever since I had tried to help him.

"My rifle! Get me my rifle! I need it!"

18

It was almost time to move, we could each feel it in our stomachs as we prepared ourselves for what was to come. My stomach gurgled and groaned uneasily and on more than one occasion I thought the contents of it was going to make an appearance, at one end or the other.

It really was a most ludicrous plan, but it was one that I was beginning to think was so that we would all be killed, so the embarrassment of a crack team of trench raiders being placed in the dock would not have to be experienced by the senior officers that created us.

Every plan that we had come up against was even more unbelievable than the last, which in some ways encouraged us to more, to be better. But this time, I wasn't feeling it as much.

I tried not to be the superstitious figure that I had often warned myself against, but the lightweight feel of my top pocket was completely unavoidable. It felt like I had lost a major organ.

I wondered if the Captain was beginning to feel the

same, that without the presence of the hip flask, more than one of us was doomed to die this morning.

I could really do with a drink.

When you get back, you can find one. If you get back.

I had done some things in the last few months as a trench raider, but this one seemed the most ridiculous yet.

"You ready?" asked the Captain, as if asking us lot how we were was somehow soothing the nervousness that had settled even in his stomach. He was not normally one for nerves, not showing it in the way that he was doing anyway.

"As I'll ever be," I risked a slight smirk, trying to buoy not just his, but my own confidence.

We better be getting medals for this.

We were about to leap up where we were hiding, one by one, and dash towards where we had seen the sniper flash come from. With any luck, the sniper would assume that we were coming directly for him and he would be forced to deal with the more immediate threats that were coming towards him.

If we were able to do that successfully, then we were banking on the Canadians being just as good as they thought they were, so that as soon as the sharpshooter manoeuvred himself to take the shot at one of us, they would be able to slot him.

Then, it was simply a snatch and grab clean up operation, grabbing the rifle that was apparently so sought after and taking off back towards our lines, with our lives hopefully still intact.

All quite simple really.

The whole premise seemed like quite a fool-proof

idea, but that was before we even took into account the hundreds of regular rifles that would be trained on us from a little farther away in the German trench. We also had to consider the very real possibility of extremely accurate artillery being called down on our position within minutes.

Therefore, if we were to be successful, but more importantly escape with our lives, then we would need the whole thing to be over in about two minutes. That was the timeframe that we had planned to and would strive to work to.

I was due to be the first to move, I was not sure why, but I had silently been volunteered by everyone else that I should be the first man out. I tried to look at all the advantages of being the first one to lead the charge.

Hopefully, a figure suddenly leaping up from a hole in the middle of No Man's Land and running towards the sniper might play into my hands somewhat, as it meant that he wouldn't be expecting it.

But, other than that, I was struggling to see the positives of being the first.

As soon as I had leapt up, I would need to maintain my course, running straight towards the sniper, but also keeping my eyes peeled for another hole close by, that I could duck into at a moment's notice.

What if there is nothing as I stand up? What if I get hit?

I was not feeling confident in the slightest, especially as I knew that the Germans would somehow be able to see the fact that this was my first time running without my talisman. I was running on very little hope.

"Andrew, you ready for this?"

Weakly, I nodded.

"Keep your head up, scout around. Make sure we are able to see where you go down. Don't worry, you'll be fine."

I wondered if he could tell that I knew he was lying.

"Yes, Sir."

"Good luck, Ellis."

"Thanks, Sir."

I couldn't say anymore than that. My mouth was bone dry. The sky was suddenly awfully quiet. I was about to go.

"When you're ready, Andrew."

A sharp exhale of breath. A quick prayer. Boldly, off I went.

~

MY FEET CRUNCHED and splashed over absolutely anything that had been left behind, by either army, in recent months. There were rifles and empty uniforms, dead comrades and the occasional rat. I pushed everything from my mind, especially as I almost tripped up on a dead Tommy, whose outstretched arm threatened to send me crashing down to the ground.

I looked all around me, trying to relocate the German sniper pit that we had identified a few moments before. I caught sight of it, a well-concealed and well-placed concentration of debris, which must have had a small gap in, for sniping through.

There was a series of concrete sheeting that stuck up sporadically, mixed with boulders and a single sandbag. It was the jagged edges and unconventional shape of the hideout that was making it difficult for our boys to get a clear shot on the German, as you never really knew where he was perched, until it was too late.

My knees began to creak and cracked on numerous occasions as I simply stared dead ahead of me, waiting for the muzzle flash that I was expecting to see at any second. I wondered if I would even have time to see it at all.

But, for the time being, I was alive, and so refocused my mind on the task at hand. Trying to find somewhere to put an end to all of this.

As quickly as I had emerged, I was submerging myself again, below a pile of rubble that had apparently been cobbled together to create a low wall. It wasn't the most ideal cover, the holes that let the emerging sunlight stream through big enough for a lucky round to come through. But it was ideal for the job.

We wanted the sniper to keep pinning us down, while simultaneously helping out the Canadians to get a proper bearing on their shot. They would really only have one shot before the sniper realised what was happening and disappeared for the foreseeable future.

Our job was to keep him busy, moving round every now and then to get him to change angles, in the hope that one time, as that was how confident the Canadians had been, he would make a mistake, and lift his head up just an inch or two too far, to allow Lawrence and Chester the chance to do their bit.

I darted around like I was a rugby player, avoiding tackles from every direction, which I was as I approached my low concrete wall. Except this player trying to tackle me was only a couple of inches tall and had just been fired by the German's brand-new rifle.

It whizzed past my head and I was convinced that it had whispered something to me as it had gone barrelling around in the other direction.

"Get your head down. Careful."

It was Bob.

My legs burned and ached as I slid my way to the wall, losing my footing just a foot away and being forced to scrabble the last little bit, in a desperate attempt for my life.

My rifle, which had hit the ground as I slipped, had fallen from my grasp, and the rounds that were now kicking up dirt around it were hindering me from a reunion with it.

I would simply have to wait, bide my time.

I was completely helpless as I watched Hamilton begin to surge towards me, his young, enthusiastic head appearing from the hole about a second after I had made it to the wall.

I could do nothing as I heard the rounds begin to make their way towards him and kicked dirt up by his feet.

"Come on, Hamilton. Quicker! Quicker!" he could not hear me, but the encouragement made me feel markedly better all the same.

He was now only about ten feet away from me and I was confident that the rounds that were being spat out were aimed directly at him and not at me for the time being.

I lunged for my rifle.

The sniper was quick.

Thwippp.

It was close, but not quite close enough. By the time

the sharpshooter was ready for another round, I had my rifle clutched to my chest and Hamilton had joined me at the wall.

The wall was so low that we could only afford to press our heads and shoulders up against it, the rest of our bodies curved outwards along the floor as we desperately tried to regain our breaths.

Next, was Captain Arnold, who seemed to stride more than sprint, confidence oozing in every footstep that he took. The Germans must have sensed it and were either confused by his assurance that he would live or petrified of the large figure that had suddenly emerged, as it took them a while to fire.

This time though, I did not feel as helpless, as I was able to fire off a few quick rounds, in unison with Hamilton, before the Captain too, joined us.

"Good going, chaps. This looks like a good spot. Nice choice."

There was just a touch of sarcasm hidden somewhere in his voice and I wondered if it was intentional or merely a result of his excitement.

Earnshaw was next.

I could almost hear his quivering breathing as he began to stumble his way from the shell hole that we had been in.

His fair hair was on display, poking out from the woollen hat that he had tried earnestly to pull over his scalp. No matter how hard he tried, there was always a defiant tuft or two that ignored his orders.

He charged towards us, screaming at the top of his lungs, which only slowed him down as he lost his breath.

Suddenly, he tripped up and fell and I watched as he

immediately rolled over to one side and into one of the other holes that were plentiful around this part of the world.

"Right, standby!" hollered the Captain. "Ellis, you tell us when he's up and we'll put some covering fire down for him."

It did not take long to see the defiant strands of hair once again.

"Now!"

The two other rifles behind me began to chatter, but before I had even come to the end of my roar, Earnshaw was down, sent off in an awkward cartwheel action and coming to a clatter on the ground.

The sniper had found his target and the rounds that began to hit the other side of the wall were a little bit too close for comfort.

The other two ducked back down.

"Where is he?!"

"Somewhere over there, Sir. Looked like he got hit."

As if he had heard me, Earnshaw suddenly appeared once again, and began charging forward to the sound of the sniper rounds that were closing in.

He had been hit once, I reasoned, so that meant there was a smaller chance of him being hit again, right?

"Fire! Fire!"

We did as we were told.

I fired off three rounds before he clattered in beside us.

"Ouch."

"Where are you hit?"

"In my knee, I think. It made an awful mess."

I took a look at him. He was indeed bleeding a lot from that area.

"Roll over, let me get a closer look."

"I better get a medal for this one, Sir."

Earnshaw smiled.

19

I was beginning to grow incredibly wearisome of the Germans' predictability.

There were certainly some things that I was desperate for, a barrage of artillery, however, was most definitely not one of them.

The earth around us began to shake and quiver, in much the same way that my hands had continued to, due to a lack of the paraffin. Each and every earth shudder was greater than the last, and I imagined the most basic form of life, right in the core of the earth, being disturbed by the inconsiderate shaking that was rocking his world.

It wouldn't have surprised me if some sort of tremor was felt many days later, on the other side of the world.

There was nothing that we could do, apart from clench our teeth down hard on each other, to stop ourselves from biting our tongues in two, and hope for the best.

We were showered consistently for a number of minutes, in dirt and dust and each time I tried to clear my mouth of the drying substance, my mouth found itself refilled by another mouthful of the stuff.

I tucked my chin into my chest, hoping that, if I was to be struck by a flying piece of debris, then the softer skin around my neck would be a far more favourable place to get it than on my skull. Besides, this way, I didn't have to watch to see how close the shells were landing. Not that I really needed to, I could simply guess by the aggressive shakes that were reverberating around my body.

For a while, I was concerned that maybe they would go on forever, until the point came where we must have been either blown to pieces or starved to death.

The whole thing, the hundreds of shells that must have landed around our position, was completely point-less, as we were far too close to the German frontline for the rounds to really be that effective. Even the Germans weren't brutal enough to shell their own men, especially when one of their best marksmen was lurking around in the boulders somewhere.

I hoped with all my heart that we hadn't scared him off, otherwise, everything, including Earnshaw being struck through the knee and McKay being stabbed in the arm, would have all been for nothing.

As quickly as it had all started, the shelling ceased immediately, the final shell blasting even louder and more aggressively than the last, it seemed. We sat in a perfect silence for about five minutes, letting the dust that had settled on our tongues seep in unwelcome, before we finally had the guts to sort ourselves out.

My ears were ringing for the next few minutes, and not one of us looked or spoke at each other for the time being, until we knew that everything was as back to as close to normal as was possible.

"Okay?" I mouthed at the others, timidly raising my thumb up, worried how much it would be shaking. But it remained steady, it gave nothing away.

One by one, the others returned a thumb and Earnshaw even managed a faint smile. I was in awe of him, and how strong he was able to be as he must have been in such pain. He had lost a lot of blood, but still he remained switched on enough to know what was going on around him and what his job was.

I tried not to think too much into how we were going to get him out of there. We would cross that bridge when we came to it.

"Close call. Maybe next time, eh?"

Oh, give me a break.

Bob's voice was slowly seeping back into my consciousness, and the ringing caused by the shells was suddenly drowned out by his shouting and taunting voice. He carried on for a good few minutes more, before he slowly began to give up.

"You've lost the hip flask now. Good. Don't think you'll last much longer without it...Well, if you aren't going to listen to me, I guess I'll just go..."

I was glad that he was gone, but at the same time, I felt a strange sense of separation begin to creep in, like I was almost starting to miss his voice when he was not there. He had been noticeably absent for a while, which had made me think it was all linked to the hip flask, but I hadn't had a sip for hours now.

Maybe there was something genuinely wrong with my brain. Maybe this was what cowardice was, a small voice in the back of your mind that slowly eats away at you, until you get to the point of no return. I wondered if McKay had had a similar voice in the back of his head, of a man that he had inadvertently got killed. I wondered if he was still there.

"Hey! Hey!"

I shuffled around uncomfortably, trying to get Bob's voice out of my head, once and for all. Or, at the very least until we had the job all wrapped up, after that he could do what he liked.

But then, as I looked across at Captain Arnold, I realised that he had heard the same thing too. Maybe I wasn't going mad after all.

"Hey! Englishman! Are you there?"

It wasn't Bob's voice at all. It wasn't a voice that I even recognised.

It was coming from the German frontline.

Hamilton was the first one to swing his rifle up and over the top of the wall.

"What can you see?" It was the question on all of our lips, but only the Captain was able to get the words out.

"Nothing. I can't see anything at all."

Hamilton jumped slightly as the voice continued to waft across the patch of ground between our wall and the sharpshooter's lair.

"Englishman! If you are still alive, you won't be for much longer. Whatever it is you are doing, you will die."

He was confident, brave even, but then again, he knew exactly where we were, and we knew where he was. He had nothing to lose but unnerving us could be the difference between escaping with his life and having his head blown to pieces.

At the thought of his death, for the first time, I began to think of the two passengers that we had attached to us on this little excursion.

Although we had been relatively safe during the artillery bombardment, the same could not be said for the Canadians and McKay who, I supposed, were right underneath the falling shells from what I could make out.

A part of me thought that maybe they had given away their position and that the artillery had been called to deal specifically with them.

I began to yearn for a sign that they were still alive and operational, otherwise we would have to carry out an altogether different plan. We would have to come up with one first.

Hamilton, the only one who seemed brave enough to have a look over the wall, gradually lifted himself up for another look, this time without his rifle. It was a very gutsy move, one that I wasn't entirely sure I would have even considered, never mind carried out.

His face was stern and the sharp lines that defined the outlines of his face was rigid, as if every muscle in his cheeks was tensed and prepared to repel a bullet.

Crack.

Hamilton immediately slumped to the floor, quite limply and we could do nothing but look on as he slid down the face of the wall. We stared at his lifeless body for a moment, totally overwhelmed at the loss of another of our comrades. We knew that it would be coming, for one of us anyway, but the sheer exhaustion that clung to our foggy minds stopped us from feeling anything in particular.

But then, Hamilton's hands began to move, not just a gradual twitching of a dying man, but the full function of his palms as they swept their way over his head and face. He was checking himself all over.

He was fine. He wasn't hit.

He began to chuckle, a breathless giggle, as he realised that he was still alive. He had been granted a new lease of life.

"That was close," I said, totally unaware that I was still able to speak.

"Yeah..." exclaimed Hamilton, "but it didn't come from the Germans."

"What do you mean?"

"It came from behind us. It must have been the Canadians."

"Did you insult one of them, Hamilton?" Earnshaw asked, his face growing paler by the minute.

"That must mean they're still operational. We carry on as planned."

"Understood, Sir."

We sat for a few moments, unsure of what to do next. A few seconds before, we thought that the sharp-shooter would have scarpered at the sight of us and then one of our comrades had been killed. But in the space of half a second, everything had changed, we were back on. We were to carry on with the original plan, if you could call it a plan. It was more of an eccentric and psychotic cobbling together of ideas than a plan as such.

"Right, come on then. We've come this far. Don't you think we should do this last little bit?"

We all knew that the Captain was right, however

much we did not want him to be. I nodded my head enthusiastically, the other two not quite so much.

"Earnshaw, with your leg, you better stay here. Give us some covering fire if you can though. Just try not to hit us, okay?"

"Absolutely, Sir. I need at least one of you to carry me back to our lines anyway."

"Ellis, you first. Then me and Hamilton. That sound okay?"

"Perfect, Sir."

"Mills Bombs at the ready, chaps."

We were all very appreciative of the Captain's efforts to obtain some of these powerful new explosives for us. The Mills Bomb had only been in service for a number of weeks, but we had already heard plenty about them, and their effectiveness. So much so that we were now ecstatic to use them.

I kept one pressed into my palm solidly, my left hand preparing to pull the pin out the second that I leapt over the wall. I would toss it ahead of me, in the general direction of the sniper's lair, in the hope that at the very least it would act as some sort of distraction. I just hoped that I wasn't as fast at running as the seven-second time delay, otherwise there was a possibility that I would end up like one of the victims of the success stories we had heard. In the best-case scenario, I could expect to come away without either of my legs.

Crack.

"That was definitely from Lawrence."

"Better get a move on then, Ellis."

I wasted no time in acknowledging the Captain, but instead threw myself around as I leapt up from behind the wall, simultaneously pulling the pin out from the small handheld bomb. My rifle swinging by my side in my left hand, I relinquished my grip on the bomb and felt the lever ping upwards. I hesitated for half a second more, before sending it into the sky, arcing towards the hideout that I was making for.

The rocks and concrete up ahead were jagged and uneven, which, despite the fact that I was gaining ground and coming considerably closer, was still difficult to make out as a laying up point.

From behind me somewhere, I heard a grunt and knew instantly that it had to be Captain Arnold pulling himself to his feet so that he could follow in my footsteps. I was relieved, as now I was not a lone target. My chances of being hit had just halved.

Either the Germans that were on their morning stand-to were blind, or every single one of their weapons had jammed as, for at least five seconds, there was not a single round sent in our direction. They must have been sitting there in total disbelief at the figures who charged towards them.

The sharpshooter's pit jutted out of the German frontline by about ten yards, on a slightly higher area of the land, which I assumed was connected to the main frontline by a shallow trench that had been hastily dug in the middle of the night. Not too dissimilar to Lawrence and Chester's hideout, I assumed.

The Mills Bomb exploded in a perfect dust cloud and I was sure that I heard a shriek come from somewhere, but I wasn't entirely certain if it was my own mind playing tricks on me. I still felt like I was carrying Bob along with me somehow.

If I had wounded, or killed the sharpshooter, then I would need to get there sharpish. I didn't want him having the opportunity to crawl away to safety, or even for a party of Germans to be in the pit when I got there, clearing out the hide of weapons and intelligence.

We had come too far now to head back to our lines empty handed.

As I got within spitting distance of my target, the first few rifles cracks began to resound, kicking dirt up around my feet.

But they were too late. I was almost there. I just hoped that the Captain and Hamilton would have as much luck as I had done.

20

The guns that were firing away and chipping at the dirt around my feet became nothing to me anymore, I had become so focused on reaching my target. I was so determined to get there, that the thought crossed my mind that I might in fact get to the pit, only to discover that I was riddled with bullet holes and in my final few moments.

I was that fuelled by excitement and intrigue.

I leapt over the jagged and uneven concrete wall that had been erected by the snipers, just catching my shin on a shard of glass that had been embedded into the top of it. My leg screamed with agony as I felt the early morning air just bite into the wound, increasing the pain that raced up my shin.

I barely had time to register what had happened to me, the blood that was now dripping from my leg of no real consequence or concern, as I had something else to do, something far more immediate and important to me right now.

My chest heaved under duress as I quickly looked about me, to see what was going on. My lungs felt as though that at any moment they may simply give up, as they constricted and wheezed in a desperate plea to the rest of my body to just slow down, for a moment.

But I couldn't listen to the demands of my body, I could not even listen to the demands of my own mind. Both of these facets of my being would do nothing to help me do what I had come here to do, they would merely push me into a corner, to hide until help arrived. I had to override the natural state of my being to run away and find the safest area possible. It was a feeling that I had taken control of many times before and was expecting myself to do once again.

You're the first one here. You are the only one here.

All these thoughts raced through my mind quicker than light itself, and I had only been in the pit for less than three seconds by the time that I began to register the guns outside firing away.

I could hear the more distinctive, more baritone voice of the Lee-Enfield sparking up some way behind me and I assumed that the two pursuing figures behind had stopped momentarily to reply to the guns that had opened up all around them.

I hoped that they would be okay.

But, for now, I was on my own here. Whatever was here, would have to be dealt with by me and me alone.

The sniper's pit that I had landed in was laid out in a worryingly similar pattern as the Canadian's own and, for a few moments, I wondered if Lawrence had been over here himself to take a look. The ground all around was covered with old sack cloths, that looked as though they had carried everything from coffee beans to love letters from Hamburg.

Over towards one side, the side that I had flown through from, and where the pit faced out into No Man's Land, there were two sacks that had been built up over many different layers, offering a dry and more comfortable firing platform for the snipers.

My assumption about the pit had been correct, trailing from behind it was a small trench, that looked so shallow that it was conceivable that it had been dug out with a small spoon or even a butter knife. It would be along that scraped-out hole that the friends of the sniper would soon come scurrying along, so I would have to be quick.

There were two bodies in the pit, one lying down quite graciously, and not moving a muscle, the other just dusting himself off as he sorted himself out after the Mills bomb had burst not too far away.

The figure that did not move, must have been the sniper himself, as he clutched hold of his wooden rifle, as if it was the only thing that held any meaning in his life. It probably was, to the point where I felt quite bad that I would have to prise it from his deathly grasp in a few moments.

First of all, however, I would have to deal with the sniper's observer, his best friend, who was still very much alive.

Covered in an even and all-encompassing layer of dirt and dust, the observer looked quite ghoulish as he began to realise what was happening. A small trickle of blood was just washing away at the worst of the dirt, as it fell from just under his hairline in a quaint raindrop that rolled across the surface of his face.

Against the backdrop of the white dust, it burned a vibrant scarlet, and, for a moment, I thought it looked almost beautiful. As he began to regroup and get himself together however, I knew that I must ignore it, and focus on finishing this chap off as well.

Outside, the gunfire increased and a Maxim gun, the distinctive knocking noise as it released its fury sounding out, joined in for good measure. I could do nothing for Captain Arnold and Hamilton now. They were good enough to know how to hold their own. Besides, I was the one with the most important job to do now. They couldn't be relying on me all the time.

The observer began to struggle to his feet, but I quickly took my opportunity and fell on him, bringing the butt of my rifle down into his mouth firmly. His mouth widened for a moment, and I felt the end of my rifle almost slide into his throat as he accepted the abuse that I put upon him.

I felt several of his teeth crack and snap under the weight, his mouth immediately gushing with blood as I pulled the rifle back for another go.

He had no weapons from what I could see and had come at me with nothing more than his fists.

Bad move.

I had learnt over the months that to go at a man with nothing apart from your knuckles was a guaranteed way to a one-way ticket to the next life. Anything, and I mean anything, is a better weapon than just the flesh of your skin.

A pencil can be thrust in an eye, a book can be used

over the head, even a drawing pin can be used as a moment of diversion by jabbing it in where it isn't wanted.

The observer had more or less signed his own death warrant. It was like he had wanted to die.

I brought the rifle butt down on him hard once again, giving him just enough time to close his mouth and turn his head to one side. I felt his jaw crack and splinter in much the same way as his teeth had done and dislodged it almost perfectly from its housing.

This chap wasn't going to be giving any motivational speeches anytime soon. Nor was he going to be calling out for his comrades, which interested me even more.

His face seemed to cave in for a split second and his skin tore apart like a piece of sodden paper, a gush of red splashing onto my face as I clobbered him.

I needed a new tactic, as I didn't much like the idea of simply clubbing a man to death, when I had much better and more humane options at my disposal. Besides, I didn't want to tire my arms out any more than was strictly necessary.

I was now confidently straddling myself over him, one leg sitting on either side of his lower abdomen, as I began to fumble around with my webbing, trying desperately to find my bayonet. If I had been a bit more alert, I probably would have fixed my bayonet long before I even began my charge, but, being the downright stupid soldier that I was, I hadn't even given it a thought.

I took some comfort from the fact however that neither the Captain nor Hamilton had cared to think about it either.

It took some fiddling to get it out but thankfully, the

German was too busy spitting out bloody teeth and other bits of matter that had been dragged in courtesy of my rifle. I was even tempted to take a look at the butt of my Lee-Enfield, expecting to see his teeth marks as I had dragged it in and out again.

Lifting the bayonet free from its sheath, I raised it up to my face, high enough so that I could get a good enough force down on the German, but not so high that I came back down with a bullet through my palm.

But just as I was about to start my descent, a shadow passed over me, a human shadow.

For a moment, I felt like Abraham, as he was about to plunge the knife down on his own son, only to be interrupted by a divine being at the last moment.

But it wasn't God who called my name that morning, it wasn't even a divine being.

"Hello, Andrew. How are you getting on? Not a good time?"

I could think of better, Bob.

Even in death, he had managed to retain his childlike features, his soft, blemish-less face a picture of serenity and innocence. He was still the slim, innocent-eyed young man that I had known when he was alive, but yet there was something different about him, and not just the fact that I knew he was not there.

It was the first time that I had seen him properly since that fateful night, the one where I had watched him spit blood in my direction as the rounds entered his body. I had looked straight into his emerald-green eyes as the life that was in him was slowly breathed out and all onto the floor of the French countryside.

His hands fell limply down by his sides, the dirtied

nails that had housed a weeks' worth of grime under them still maintaining its grasp in the real world. His hands hung solemnly, not taking any notice of the one thing that had drawn my attention.

The tunic that he wore was the same colour that it always had been, khaki green, but to one side, over his left hip to be exact, there was a dark red stain that dripped intermittently from the hem of his uniform.

That was the wound that I had inflicted upon him, that was the one thing that had led to him being killed. If it hadn't been for me shooting him, then the injury would never have split open, the stitches giving way under the strain of war.

If none of that had happened, then Bob Sargent would have been able to move a lot faster and out of trouble. He would still be alive today, and not just in my head.

"You could look a bit more pleased to see me," he said, giving me a bloody-toothed grin. "You thought I was dead."

You are dead, Bob.

"Come on, I'm really thirsty, Andrew. Surely you can give me a bit of that drink? You never shared it with me before. Come on, don't you think I deserve it?"

Leave me alone.

I was well aware that he was not there, he was just a figment of my imagination, but for some reason, I could not take my gaze off him, I could not even blink. I was transfixed by the apparition at the top of the sniper's pit.

"You don't have it, do you?"

You know full well that I don't.

"What a shame, I—"

At that moment a gunshot erupted, and a searing

pain filled my entire being. Bob, who had been stood quite proudly above the hole that I was in, suddenly fell backwards, a series of bullets hitting his chest like they had done a few weeks before. He spat his blood towards me, before he disappeared somewhere out in No Man's Land.

Instantly, I turned my attention back to the German, and the pain that had suddenly exploded somewhere in my body.

I had made a mistake.

The German had not been planning to fight with just his fists, but with a small knife that he had managed to withdraw while I was staring up at Bob. Bob had only been there for about two seconds, but that was all that was needed for the German to find his knife and stick it in my arm somewhere.

I could still not see exactly where it was. All I could see was blood.

As quick as flash, I felt the cold steel dagger that he had clutched in between his fingers, as it slid its way forcefully into my thigh, the largest and most obvious target for the man who lay beneath me.

I roared a roar that a wounded tiger would have been proud of, as I clutched at the wound that had sent me into oblivion.

I felt weak all of a sudden, as the German suddenly overpowered me and threw me off him. I could do nothing except stare at the blood that now gushed from my body, with the same apparent obsession as I had stared at Bob.

I knew that I had to do something else, but the fact

remained that I simply couldn't do it. Something was stopping me.

The wound was deep, and I could feel it start to burn as the fire was lit elsewhere in my upper leg. I became cold all of a sudden, apart from in my thigh where the heat seemed to reach a crescendo.

I tried to keep it as still as possible, so that I didn't accidentally spill some blood that might come in handy later on, but it was no use. The wound was burning so badly it felt as though some sort of liquid flame was being burned directly into the cut itself.

I continued to lose all sense of power and determination to get out, just as I watched the German come at me again, from the other side of the hole, once he had regained his breath.

21

I didn't know exactly how the German ended up dead, the only important thing was that he was. He lay beside me in a mixture of my blood and his, slowly rolling his eyes around the back of his head as if he had simply become a doll.

From where I was, I could see no wounds exactly, but he clutched at his chest with an adamant look upon his face. Slowly, solemnly, he reluctantly relinquished his grip on his chest, as he slowly began to lose the will to live.

He died a few seconds later, staring straight into my eyes.

Just as the German observer breathed his last, a figure appeared at the top of the hole, his features robbed by the brilliant sunshine that now lit up the entire world around me. Quickly, he slid down into the pit, followed by another, equally concerned for my welfare.

It must have been the others, although I could barely remember their names or recall their faces any longer.

They began to pull me around rather urgently, but I was beginning to lose my care for everything in the world.

I looked around for Bob, the rather ominous and demanding character who had been standing on top of the hole just a few seconds before.

Come here, Bob. I can give you a drink. I'm sorry.

I caught sight of a face that I recognised, the wild expression in Captain Arnold's eyes the least of my worries at that moment in time. I wanted to see Bob, especially as it could quite well be my last time.

I found my arms being ripped open, prised apart, to which I noticed that it was Hamilton, the inexperienced and ambitious young man who had lowered himself to the ranks, to be able to fight in this awful bloodbath of a war.

"Hamilton..." I rasped, instantly closing my mouth due to the shockwaves of pain that went shooting through my chest.

I looked down at what it was that he wanted, to which I was caught by a gasp of surprise at what lay cradled on my chest.

It was the rifle. The very rifle that we had been tasked with retrieving and bringing back to our lines as intelligence. I stared at it, like a child stares at a newly-bought toy for a while, marvelling at its every groove and polished mechanism.

I toyed with it for a few moments more, before I began to make out voices in my blood-filled ears.

"We need to move, soon."

"Get the rifle, I think we're going to have to leave him."

I heard the voices, but could not quite register them,

as I no longer knew what was real and what was just my imagination any longer.

As I listened to the two men going about their business, checking me over for anymore leaking holes and trying to get the bounty from my grasp, I noticed a third man standing behind them. This figure stood tall, unlike the others who were crouched down low to avoid becoming a rifleman's dream.

This man simply stood there watching and for a second, I thought he wore a German uniform, although I could not be sure.

I smeared my blood all over the rifle, before gripping incredibly tightly onto the sight that was perched on top of it. That was what we had come for, and I was not going to let it go.

"Sergeant, I need you to let go of it. Come on."

"No!"

"Let go of it, Andrew. Let go. I have. Why can't you?"

"Bob?"

He was back, this time with a more welcoming, but still bloodied, smile, which was warmly reciprocated. I wondered for a brief second if this was where I was due to die. I had seen many other men pass on into the next life, where a number of them had died with a smile on their face. I could never tell what made a man do that, but in that moment, I realised, that maybe, as you fade out of one world, you are granted a brief vision of the next, with the one person that you have been missing the most.

"Bob," I muttered, still staring at the standing figure, "it is good to see you again. I'm sorry."

"I know, Andrew. I know."

He looked at me pitifully for a few more seconds, before simply turning around and walking back out of the pit, quite as if nothing had happened at all.

At that moment in time, I suddenly felt incredibly alone.

Eventually, I began to think about the pain, and realised that the whole time I had been with Bob, I hadn't given it a second thought. The moment that I did begin to register it in my legs, I immediately wished that Bob would return.

I bellowed and roared, much to my own embarrassment, as I suddenly became aware of the fact that I was still a sergeant in the British army, and they never died a coward's death. At least they weren't meant to.

I bit down hard on the backs of my teeth, so hard that I felt them bury themselves further into my gums.

My legs continued to feel like they had been placed on a spit and were slowly being roasted to the point where I would pass out.

Gradually, it seemed like the best option for me, as I was having to put a great deal of effort into simply staying awake.

The edges of my vision suddenly became warped, and the longer that I had to think about it, the more I realised that my world was turning into a funny kind of grey. I was losing colour from everything, to the point where even my blood was nothing more than a bit of a darker patch on my being.

Captain Arnold continued to try and work a bandage around my legs, tying them so tightly that I thought he was trying to strangle my limbs.

"I reckon this is a Blighty injury, what do you say, Sarge?"

I didn't know what to reply to the young Hamilton. If he was right, then I couldn't wait. Maybe I would make a full recovery and get to see my family again. I was particularly looking forward to meeting my sister again, the one who used to take great enjoyment out of jumping in lakes rather too close to me. Maybe then I would even remember what she looked like.

I promised myself never to forget her again. I was going to write to her as soon as I made it back.

If...you make it...back.

I was getting tired. Too tired to carry on looking into Hamilton's eyes.

"Sir, he's going, we need to move...and now."

"Mills Bombs, Hamilton. Have you got them?"

Everything began to grow darker as well as greyer.

"Yes, Sir."

"That way, when I say, okay? Then we make a run for it with the Sergeant here."

Everything went black.

"Ready?"

"Ready."

"Okay. Now."

There was a sudden eruption of noise, but I could not bring my eyes to widen so that I could see what was going on, let alone lend them a hand.

I began to mutter, under my breath at first, but then much more clearly, at least I thought so.

"The rifle...have you got it? The rifle? Where is it?"

I got no response.

Oh well.

You only have yourself to blame.

I wasn't sure why I thought that. Maybe it was because of the paraffin that Bob had appeared and distracted me. Or maybe it had been because I had failed to admit to myself that I was too tired to carry on anymore.

The only thing that I was certain of, was that Bob had almost got me killed.

You're not out of the woods yet.

"I'm thirsty, Andrew."

"There's nothing left, Bob. I'm sorry. I have nothing left."

I had no paraffin. It was all gone.

As the noises around me gradually went the same way of my vision, I became certain of only one thing.

Oh, how I really needed that hip flask.

THE END
Andrew Ellis and the team return in 'Clouded Judgement' - Book 5 in the Trench Raiders series. Available on Amazon now!

YOU CAN HELP MAKE A DIFFERENCE

Reviews are one of my most powerful weapons in
generating attention for my books.
Unfortunately, I do not have a blockbuster budget when
it comes to advertising but
Thanks to you I have something better than that.

Honest reviews of my books helps to grab the attention of
other readers so, even if you have one minute, I would be
incredibly grateful if you could leave me a review on
whichever Amazon store suits you.

Thank you so much.

GET A FREE BOOK TODAY

If you enjoyed this book, why not pick up another one, completely free?

'Enemy Held Territory' follows Special Operations Executive Agent, Maurice Dumont as he inspects the defences at the bridges at Ranville and Benouville. Fast paced and exciting, this Second World War thriller is one you won't want to miss!

Simply go to:

www.ThomasWoodBooks.com/free-book
To sign up!

ABOUT THE AUTHOR

Thomas Wood is the author of the 'Gliders over Normandy' series, The Trench Raiders, as well as the upcoming series surrounding Lieutenant Alfie Lewis, a young Royal Tank Regiment officer in 1940s France.

He posts regular updates on his website
www.ThomasWoodBooks.com

and is also contactable by email at
ThomasWoodBooks@outlook.com

twitter.com/thomaswoodbooks
facebook.com/thomaswoodbooks

Printed in Great Britain
by Amazon

51012616R00104